Copyright © 2017 by Ashe Moon

2023 - 2nd Edition

All rights reserved. No part of this publication may be reproduced, distributed, or transmitted in any form or by any means, including photocopying, recording, or other electronic or mechanical methods, without the prior written permission of the publisher, except in the case of brief quotations embodied in critical reviews and certain other noncommercial uses permitted by copyright law.

WED TO THE OMEGA

THE LUNA BROTHERS MPREG ROMANCE SERIES

Stay updated with sales and new releases by subscribing to Ashe Moon's personal newsletter! Scan the QR code below with your phone camera!

* * *

If you're looking for something a little more personal you can also join my private Facebook group, **Ashe Moon's Ashetronauts**!

My group is a safe space to chat with me and other readers, and where I also do special exclusive giveaways and announcements. Hope to see you there!

THE LUNA BROTHERS SERIES

Vander's Story - Doctor to the Omega
Christophe's Story - Marked to the Omega
Arthur's Story - Bound to the Omega

TRESTEN

The weathered stone halls of every school building within the Dawn Academy were lined with records of the wolves who had come before—clan leaders, genius minds, master warriors, and all the greatness that lay in between.

I strolled down the main hall of the Fighting Arts School, my hand outstretched towards the wall. I extended my fingers every time I passed the portrait of an omega, touching the cool metal name plaques beneath their paintings. Very few omega wolves had their portraits up on those walls. I could walk the length of a full hallway and count on two hands the number of names who had the distinction of being an omega graduate in the fighting arts. Those were the few who kept my resolve burning. There was Pavlov Kirichenko, one of the very first omegas to train here nearly three hundred years ago. He went on to become a head instructor. Regenald Fienback, the great omega general. Victor Morgan, philosopher and founder of the Silver Claw style of combat. Robert Rathgard, Charles Dennis, Leonard Van Hensley... all great omegas who had excelled in an alpha's world.

I belonged here, just like they had.

I was confident in my abilities. I knew I was one of the best fighters in the entire school—but because I was an omega, I only got constant shit from my alpha peers. And to make things worse, I recently got my mark—a streak of black in my otherwise white hair.

"Hey."

I turned and sighed when I saw Loch Luna sauntering out from whatever dark corridor he'd been hiding in. Loch had his own cooldown routine, usually doing dumb shit like holding a one-armed handstand for thirty minutes while shirtless, just to show off to the alpha females. He had his shirt draped over his shoulder now, his stupidly ripped torso shiny with sweat. What a joke.

"What do you want, Loch?" I said, not stopping. I just wanted to be left alone.

He flashed that killer smile of his, his fangs glinting in the dusty sunlight streaming in through the huge hallway windows.

. . .

"Tresten. Good fighting last class," he said, falling into step beside me.

"Thanks. You had some good matches too. Even though you still take way too long to shift."

"I'm what, half a second slower than you are? Not everyone can speed-shift like you."

"You've always been a step behind me, even when we were younger."

"Oh, is that right? I could've sworn *you've* gotten slower."

"Hah. In your dreams."

He pointed to the streak in my hair. "Is that making it harder for you?"

"Why don't you go chew a bone," I grunted.

"I'm serious. Like, honestly curious."

I gave him a sharp look. "You think this would make it any harder for me to kick your ass?"

. . .

"It means you're in heat, right? You know, I've heard the reason why there are so few omega graduates from the FAS is because most end up finding an alpha and dropping out. I mean, being in heat and surrounded by hot blooded alphas all day…"

I bit back a surge of irritation. "So sorry to distract you. Is that why you're so weak? Can't deal with being around an omega in heat? Or are all Crescent Moon Pack alphas that slow."

He snorted. "Trust me, no Ice River Pack omega could ever faze me."

"Just *beat* you, then?"

"I won't downplay your abilities. You did, but you *were* slower than usual."

We entered into the training gymnasium: a gigantic, circular dirt floored arena in the very center of the Fighting Arts School. A huge dome skylight allowed the sun to pour into the ring, and was sometimes opened to allow the natural elements to come in. Training in the snow or rain was always an interesting challenge.

. . .

Without another word, Loch split off and went to greet a group of young alphas who were huddled around a laptop computer, probably watching fighting technique videos. I went to my usual spot against the wall to do some quick warm ups before the next class. All around the middle of the arena, people were training or in the middle of sparring matches, and I watched as a practice fight commenced. The two fighters were stripped down to skintight underwear, since anything looser wouldn't meld with their bodies as they commenced the shift. They burst into a ferocious sprint towards one another and then leapt into the air, their bodies shapeshifting into a half wolf form—a common fighting technique which gave them the dexterity of a bipedal style mixed with the ferocity and natural weapons of their wolf. The two clashed and kicked up a cloud of dirt, and I watched with mild interest, noting about fifteen critiques I had with their technique.

My eyes went back to Loch, who said something to make the group around him laugh. I took my shirt off and began to stretch my muscles. I was alone in my area, but that was fine. I was used to it, and that was how I liked it. No alpha wanted to associate with an omega—especially one who had a mark. They thought it would make them softer.

You've gotten slower. Loch's voice echoed in my head.

I unconsciously touched my fingers to the dark streak in my hair. Stupid Loch.

. . .

At 22, he was two years older than me and hardly what I'd call a friend—and yet we'd been around each other since childhood, simply because of the relationship between our two clans: the Ice River Pack and the Crescent Moon Pack. My family headed the Ice River Pack, and Loch's the Crescent Moons, and there was a generations-long rivalry between us. Loch and I were born into a peace truce set in place by our parents. We grew up feeling the tensions of our clans' past, knowing that just a single generation ago, there was violence between us.

There was a loud crack, the sound of muscle on muscle, and my attention turned back to the fighters. One hurtled to the ground, his snout buried in the dirt as he slid on his face. The other stood over him, fangs bared, paws spread out wide at his side with claws out. The match was over. Fur melded back into flesh, and they were soon in human form again. The winner put out a hand and helped the other up to his feet. His face was caked with dirt, and he laughed as his friend patted him on the back.

The doors to the arena burst open, and everyone rose to attention as Master Graffer strode in, his traditional battle robe billowing behind him. "Ladies and gentlemen!" His voice boomed out, filling up the entire cavernous arena.

I hurried out to the center where the rest of the class was gathering in organized formation. Master Graffer paced back and forth until everyone was standing at attention, and then held out his fist in front of him, clasping his open palm over it. The class returned the gesture. It was our martial salute, representing the fusion of man and beast.

"Let's pick up where we left off and get into some more matches, shall we? Who wants to go first?"

Loch's hand shot up first, and then mine.

"Luna. Croc. You're up."

I tossed my battle robe aside and Loch did the same, and we moved to the center as the class formed a ring around the fighting area. The light from the domed window above us created a spot of light that shone onto us. It cascaded down Loch's nearly naked body, casting shadows from the rigid lines of his muscles. His physique was flawless, and seemed almost effortlessly so. Being born with the advantage of physical strength was the benefit of being an alpha. It was something I had to work my ass off to achieve, and even then, my physical strength would always be a step behind his —and every other alpha.

I needed to rely on my other abilities—like my speed and dexterity. I knew I outmatched everyone else.

"Fighters ready? No claws. Half-contact bites," Master Graffer said. "Three-minute match, an ending blow or ten second knockdown ends it."

He drew his arm up.

"FIGHT!"

I felt the brief snap of pain as my bones rearranged themselves, reforming and snapping into new configurations as I moved to a half-shift. My face exploded forward into a snout, my teeth sharpening into deadly points. My vision sharpened, and I could suddenly hear *everything*—a bird's claws against the glass skylight, the breathing of every single one of my classmates standing in the circle around us.

I focused my senses onto the sound of Loch's feet crunching through the dirt as he ran toward me. To my surprise, he was already in his half-shift form, and drawing his arm back for an attack. Shit, maybe I *was* slower.

I stepped to the right just in time to dodge his strike, and his arm grazed the fur of my cheek. Evading had left him open! I pivoted on my right leg, using my tail to aid in the speed of the turn, and opened my jaws to clamp them down on his shoulder. They snapped together, catching nothing but a tuft of fur and air. He'd dodged—

My side exploded in white hot pain, and my feet left the ground as his strike sent me flying through the air. *Fuck.*

Everything spun when I hit the dirt. It felt like my entire skull was vibrating. My ears perked. I heard his rapid steps across the ground—*get up, here he comes. Left!*

I rolled right, just in time to miss his clawed foot stamping down onto the ground. *Shift! Shift!* When I got up, I was in full wolf form. I had to sacrifice strength for speed, because there was no question about it. I'd gotten slower. Not just the shift transition, but my overall speed—

Loch's foot tore through the dirt towards my face, kicking up a spray of sand. I leapt to the side, barely dodging him. I may have gotten slower, but Loch still had a tendency to put too much power into his attacks, leaving himself open—and that was what he'd done now. *Forward!* I lowered my head and shot into him, bashing the hard part of my skull into his stomach.

Loch stumbled backwards with a grunt. My head was ringing, but I wasn't going to give him any time to react. I was on him in a second, jaws open and fangs at his throat.

"Halt!" Master Graffer called. "Match! Killing blow, match goes to Tresten."

"Fuck," Loch growled.

. . .

I hopped away from him, and we both shifted back to human form. "How was that?" I asked him. "Slow enough for you?"

He shot me a glare, his ruby eyes glinting in the sunlight.

"Work on your control, Loch," Master Graffer said. "Don't throw all your power into your attacks. Look for balance. Tresten, nice turnaround." I waited for him to make a comment about my speed, but he said nothing.

One of Loch's buddies tossed him his robe, and he slapped palms with a couple of the guys as he joined them in the circle. My robe sat alone in the dirt, and I scooped it up and shook it out before putting it back on. There were no congratulatory pats on the back for me. Nobody said a word to me.

"Who's fighting next?"

Hands went up.

"Bellock. Lenford. Your match."

Bellock and Lenford? That was just about the most uneven pairing I could think of. Stell Lenford was my age, and small for an alpha. A son from a low family in a low status clan, he'd always been slower, weaker, and softer than everyone else in the school. Martin Bellock, on the other hand, was from the Blood Gulch Clan. They were a newer clan on the rise—his father had started the pack after making millions on an iffy nutritional supplement pill that was supposed to make you shift bigger and tougher. Who knows if it actually worked, but if it did, then Martin had to have been scarfing those pills down since he was a baby.

The class moved to form a ring around the fighting area, while Martin and Stell took center, stripping off their battle robes and shoes. Martin towered over Stell, his body bulging with so much muscle that he looked like he'd fit in better with a bear clan. His gaze was vicious and vacant—probably the worst combination to have. He grinned stupidly at Stell, showing off his canines, and pointed a meaty finger at him. Stell glared back.

Silent tension gripped the room, as we all waited for Master Graffer to commence the match. He swung his hand in a downward arc. "Begin!"

Martin barreled forward, shouting out a yell that warped into a ferocious roar as his body shifted. Fur exploded from his skin. Bones cracked and popped as they expanded and moved. His face pulled forward into a partial snout, and his already expansive muscles burst out with tense veins. He was in a bipedal half-shift, charging towards Stell

Stell was still in human form. He dove forward and somersaulted easily between Martin's legs, and then began to shift. Martin turned, slobber dripping from his gnash of fangs, and bellowed an angry roar. Stell moved past the half-shift form. He was going full wolf—he knew he was down on strength against Martin, so he would rely on speed. But would it be enough? Martin had shit agility because of his size, but Stell was no sprinter himself.

Martin charged at him, swung a meaty hand—

Stell dodged! He kicked off from the dirt with his hind legs and sailed through the air, up and over Martin's body. Landing behind him, Stell wasted no time. He sprung forward and threw himself against Martin's calf, knocking the brute down to one knee. Then he went straight for the neck, jaws wide.

He never made it. With surprising speed, Martin thrust out a hand and nabbed Stell midair by the throat. The class let out a collective groan as Martin slammed Stell onto the ground in a cloud of dust. An impact like that was a sure knock-out.

"Thought you could get me, you little bitch?" Martin growled. Then he turned and laid a fist into Stell's motionless body.

"Match!" Master Graffer shouted.

. . .

Martin didn't stop. He laid into him, blood matting fur. A screen of dust tinged the air. Loch and a couple others stepped forward to intervene, but Master Graffer was faster. The dust settled. Master Graffer stood in between the two; he'd caught Martin's monstrous fist in his open, still-human palm.

"I said, ENOUGH," he bellowed, and took a single step forward with his right foot. This tiny movement sent Martin stumbling back onto the ground. He stared with that piercing, vacant gaze of his, a wicked smile curled on his lips. His tongue lolled out and licked the blood from his face. Then he shifted back to human form.

Master lifted Stell up to his paws. He was conscious, but bleeding from one ear. "I'm alright," he grumbled, shifting back. He limped his way back to the circle.

"Lenford, good strategy, but you were too hasty in your attack and left yourself open. Bellock? Control."

Martin snorted. His buddies chuckled.

"No honor," Loch mumbled. "No honor at all."

"Next fight!"

* * *

After class ended, I made my way from the Fighting Arts School to the library that lay at the center of the Dawn Academy campus. After watching the gruesome match between Martin and Stell, one thing had stuck in my mind:

Would I have been able to evade Martin?

I kept on seeing the moment his hand snatched Stell from the air and pummeled him to the ground. I'd matched with Martin before and had plenty of victories, but the fight with Loch had put doubt into my mind. I *did* feel slower.

My mark had appeared about a week ago, signaling the change that had occurred in my body. I'd known what it meant, of course, but I'd still been surprised by the changes that I couldn't physically see. My reaction time felt bogged down. I was easily fatigued. My shift speed had slightly diminished. But the worst change had to do with my sense of smell.

I could *smell* alphas now, in a way that I never had been able to before. I could smell their scent drifting off of them like a starving man could smell a meal in the oven. The thing that disturbed me was that I was sure they could smell me too. I occasionally caught a few of my fellow students giving me odd looks as I passed them in the hallways, or staring at me during training. I was used to being stared at as an omega in the FAS—but unfriendly stares. Not stares like these.

. . .

There was only one person who I wanted to talk to about this, one person who would know if I was going to keep getting weaker. I sent her a text message asking where she was, even though I already knew, and sure enough, she replied back with a single word: "Library."

Velvy Harte was a student at the Historical Studies School at the Dawn Academy. She was a beta, and she was my best friend. In fact, she was the only friend I had.

I climbed the spiraling staircase up to the fifth floor of the library where Velvy liked to hang out, and found her sitting at a desk with a laptop, surrounded by towering stacks of old books. She wrinkled her nose and looked up from her computer as I took the seat across from her.

"Tresten, you stink like an unwashed battle robe. I could practically smell you the moment you walked into the building."

I lifted my arm and wafted my hand under my armpit, grinning. Velvy cringed and covered her face. "You suck," she said.

"I need to ask you something, Velvy," I said, leaning in secretively. She raised an eyebrow and closed her laptop. I pointed to the streak going through my hair. "What do you know about omegas in heat?"

. . .

"Well, I'm not an expert in shifter physiology or anything like that."

"But you must've read a book or two about it?"

"I read all twelve volumes of Levtone's *Shifter Medicine*. That's about it."

That's about it. I laughed. "Okay, I think that just about qualifies you as an expert in my book."

"What do you want to know?"

"What are the symptoms of an omega going into heat?"

She eyed me like a disappointed school teacher being asked a dumb question. "The mark in the hair and fur," she said, reaching out and poking my head. "An increased desire to want to…" She cleared her throat. "Drag an alpha into your bed."

"Yeah, but what about performance changes? Lately I haven't been feeling quite myself, and others are noticing."

. . .

"That's normal," she said. "I don't remember exactly; I'd have to get the book to tell you, but you should expect some fatigue."

"How long is this supposed to last?" I wasn't sure I wanted to hear the answer.

"Well… I'm quite certain it will last until your 'season' is over. So—"

"Thirty years, or my first child," I groaned. "*Fuck.*" I had absolutely no plans to find a mate, much less have a kid, right now. I was the only child, so of course it was expected of me in order to stay head of the clan… but I only had one thing on my mind right now, and that was the FAS. I wanted to graduate with glory. I wanted my face on the wall of the school. How could I do that in a weakened state?

"What's the matter? Having trouble beating people up?" She laughed.

"Not funny, Velvy," I said. "You know what this means for me."

"I know. I'm sorry. Your father never told you any of this? He's an omega."

. . .

"He never told me about being crippled by it. He only warned me about the potential shit I'd get from my fellow students. Besides, Dad studied the medicinal arts. He wasn't a fighter."

"Your other father never said anything?"

My other father, who I called Pa, was an alpha and had been a champion at the FAS back in his day, and was still very well known amongst the faculty at the Dawn Academy for the massive donations he made to the school. He'd always encouraged me to become a fighter, never once giving me a word of discouragement. If he'd known how being in heat would affect my performance, he'd kept it to himself.

I shook my head. Velvy patted my arm. "What will you do?"

I balled my hands into tight fists, and a smile crept across my face. I wasn't a stranger to adversity. This was just a bump on my road to glory—and one that I could overcome. It'd only make every victory that much sweeter.

"Fight," I said.

Velvy and I went out to eat dinner together, and after dropping her off at her apartment, I drove back home. I still lived in my family mansion, as was customary for the son of a clan leader. Living on my own like most of my peers would've been nice, but there was tradition to uphold. I had a lot of respect for my parents and for the clan—I would do anything they asked of me—so it wasn't a problem.

I drove my car through the gate and up the winding driveway that led into our property, just as the garden lights were turned on. I always loved to see the lights come on at dusk. The events of the day were still set in my mind, and I wanted to speak to my parents about it. If there was anyone who could give me advice about this, it was them.

Pulling up my car to the front of the house, I was greeted by William, our butler.

"Master Tresten," he said with a curt nod.

"Evening, William," I said, handing over the keys.

"Your fathers request your immediate presence in Master Desmond's study."

I nodded, curious what this could be about. I couldn't remember the last time I'd had my presence immediately requested. How very official. I hurried up the steps and went inside. Two of the wait staff were there, and they greeted me and took my bag, reminding me that my parents were waiting for me in Pa's study. My mind began to turn over the possibilities. Maybe some clan duty I needed to attend to?

Some official responsibility as only son? Or maybe a death in the family…? I hoped that wasn't the case; that would be terrible. I did have an old aunt suffering from shift-stuck, where she was unable to shift back to human form. But that wasn't a fatal thing, was it?

I walked past the dining room, where I caught the warm, rich smell of roasted lamb wafting out from the kitchen. Going up the stairs, I passed the towering oil portraits of my family ancestry. Men and women standing regally with their wolf form seated next to them. I'd spent hours as a kid staring up at these paintings, fantasizing about who these people had been. Dad and Pa would tell me stories about them, sometimes, telling me that all the great things they did—and terrible things too—still lived on inside me.

I knocked on the tall double doors of Pa's study. "Dad? Pa? You wanted to see me?"

"Come in, Tresten!" Pa's voice boomed.

I pushed the door open. Pa was behind his massive desk, his enormous hands folded in front of him. Dad was sitting on the side couch—legs crossed, back straight; proper as always. He turned to look at me and smiled. "Evening, Tresten," he said, his voice like a breeze.

"Hi, Dad," I said. "Pa."

. . .

Pa stood up and gestured. "Shut the door behind you, Tresten." I did as I was told, and Pa stood stiffly behind his desk. I could tell he was forcing a smile. I looked over to Dad—his expression was even and calm. A beat of silence passed, and I would be lying if I said that I didn't feel uncomfortable.

"…Yes?" I asked hesitantly.

Pa cleared his throat. "Take a seat, son," he said. I sat in the big chair in front of his desk, across from the couch where Dad was. Pa sat back down, and then grunted and cleared his throat. He shifted in his seat. Now was I really starting to get weirded out. Pa was one of the toughest alpha males I knew. He was loud and brash, and I never saw him choke up like this.

He turned to Dad. "Julius? Can you…?"

"Tresten, we'd like to talk to you about your mark," Dad said softly.

"Okay," I said, somewhat relieved, but at the same time even more intrigued. "I was hoping to talk to you about it as well. I had questions about the changes that've been happening—"

"Questions can come later," Pa grunted. "Tresten, tell me about clan succession."

. . .

"The eldest son of the leading family inherits the rights to taking over the clan," I said. "Barring any challenges from other pack members, or rival clans."

"Good. And you're our only son, which means that the status of our family as leader of the Ice River Pack relies on your future."

"I am aware of this, Pa," I said. I had a bad feeling about where this was heading.

"Then you understand the weight of your position as an in-heat omega. The difficult truth is that the full responsibility lies on you, and as a solo omega, our family is in a vulnerable position. There will be hungry clans who will sniff out potential weakness once the time for succession has come."

I straightened. "Challenges are nothing to me, Pa. I'm *your* son. I'm one of the best in my class. Besides, we're one of the wealthiest clans in the country. Our loyal pack members would—"

"Pack members can waver," Dad spoke up, his voice still even. He stood from the couch and sat down in the chair next to me, reaching for my hand. "Even from wealth. And you by yourself would be vulnerable, no matter how strong you are."

. . .

"And you are strong," Pa agreed.

I looked back and forth between them. "What are you saying?"

Pa sighed. "I want you to know that this decision was not easy for either of us to make," he said. "We both understand what your fight training at the Dawn Academy means to you."

A cold chill went through my body.

Dad squeezed my hand. "We need to make sure our strength as leaders of the Ice River Pack is solidified. And the only way to do that, with you as our only son, is with the help of one of our allies."

"A joining of power," Pa said. "A marriage."

LOCH

*M*y cell phone ringing loudly from somewhere bolted me upright in bed. I blinked and looked around, trying to remember exactly where I was.

A moan to my left. I looked over and saw the ruffle of hair and flash of skin that was the girl I met last night. What was her name? Jennifer? Jackie? I felt bad for not remembering, but then again, she probably didn't remember mine, either.

"Mm…" she groaned, turning over. "Loch, what is that?"

Damnit.

My phone kept ringing. The last place I had it was… my pants. Which were on the floor.

. . .

WED TO THE OMEGA

Sliding out from the bed, I scooped my trousers up from the floor and pulled them on. My phone kept on ringing, and I got it out from my pocket. It was Christophe, my elder brother. I thought about letting it go to voicemail, but decided against it. Christophe was first in line to be the leader of the Crescent Moon Pack, and he took that responsibility very seriously. *Extremely* seriously. To the point where I basically had a mom and two dads. I could do without getting chewed out when I got home.

"Yeah?" I said, answering it. I picked up my button down from the floor and held the phone to my ear with my shoulder while I put my shirt on.

"Where are you?" Christophe asked.

"School," I said. It wasn't a lie—I was in someone's dorm.

"Uh huh," he said. "Get dressed and get your ass home immediately. And… try not to let anyone see you? You're a Luna. You're a representative of the Crescent Moons, and you need to act as such."

"Hey." I grinned, buttoning up my shirt. "I'm just practicing some friendly diplomatic relations with other clans."

. . .

"I don't think I need to remind you that co-ed visits aren't allowed in the Dawn Academy dorms, Loch. Get home. Mother and Father want to see you."

"Mom and Dad? What do they want?"

My new friend sat up on the bed, holding the blanket cross her chest. "Will you stop talking so loud? My RA will hear you."

I smiled and waved to her before plonking down onto the floor. *Funny; you didn't say anything about that last night.* I pulled my socks and shoes on.

"I don't know," Christophe replied in my ear. "But they're gathering the family, so it's something serious. Any trouble you've gotten into lately you need to fess up about?"

I laughed. "If there was, what would you do?"

"I'm your big brother. You can tell me about things like that."

"Right… I'll see you at home, yeah? On my way now." I disconnected the call and stuffed the phone back into my pocket.

. . .

WED TO THE OMEGA

"I'll see myself out," I told the girl whose name I still couldn't remember. Really, I should've made my exit last night. These awkward morning talks were always the worst.

"I had fun," she said. "See you around campus?"

I gave her a non-committal smile before pulling the window open and sticking my head out. It was a three-story drop—no problem. I climbed through and pushed myself out, dropping into a tight roll when I hit the ground. I brushed off my clothes and strolled towards the parking lot.

* * *

The moment I got home, Christophe ordered me to wait in the dining room while he went to gather my other two brothers, Arthur and Vander, along with my parents. The truth was, I hated being at home. The Crescent Moon Clan was one of the oldest in the country and had always been strong—but recent financial trouble had put a stress on my parents, who were already intense enough as it was, and hardly seemed to approve of anything I did.

I couldn't help but feel like a burden in some ways. Christophe and Arthur were both older than me, and both of them had graduated from the Dawn Academy. Vander was 17—nearly time to start thinking about his choice of study, and seeing as all of his older brothers had gone to Dawn, he would want to choose it too. It was my parents' alma mater, so I couldn't imagine them refusing, even though the Dawn Academy was expensive. Actually, "expensive" was a bit of an understatement; the place served only the best or wealthiest students in the world.

I was the third alpha. Christophe was in line for taking over the pack, Arthur would support as the second oldest, and I was... well, as third, I really didn't have a role. Vander was an omega, so he would always get special treatment in the family.

So, I spent as much time out of the house as I could, usually at a girl's place—even though I knew my parents frowned on it—or with one of my buddies from the FAS. Anything to relieve some of the extra burden of having to deal with me. If I could, I would just move out altogether if tradition didn't frown on it, and if I wasn't living on my parents' coin.

I strummed my fingers on the dining table, wracking my brain trying to think of something I'd done to deserve a meeting like this. The last time I'd been called for an official family meeting was... when I was eighteen, and they'd wanted to tell my brothers about my acceptance to the FAS at Dawn. Before that, it was when I was fifteen, when I was dating Sherry. She was a beta from a low born family, and of course, a high-status alpha like myself wasn't allowed to be with someone like her. I'd gotten a lecture from both my parents and Christophe, and in the end I wasn't allowed to see her again.

That whole ordeal was part of the reason why I hadn't given any further thought to serious relationships. Even when I got into Dawn, and my parents encouraged me to find someone, it was just easier to fuck around and not risk bringing home someone who'd make my parents disappointed—again. That, and the Fighting Arts School was my life now. I didn't have time for a relationship, not with my training schedule.

Whatever this was about, I couldn't imagine it was because I did something wrong. My parents might not have complete approval of how I lived my personal life, but I was hardly a trouble maker.

Still… I couldn't shake the feeling that whatever news I was going to receive was not going to make me happy.

After ten minutes, the doors to the dining room opened. I turned around to look at the entrance, and I watched my three brothers filed in, with Christophe at the front. I was at the end of the table, and the three of them took the seats adjacent to me. Christophe sat straight backed, his glasses perched on the bridge of his nose, looking proper as always. Arthur looked distracted and in his own thoughts. Van put his bare feet up on the edge of the table and tilted his chair back.

"Sooo… what the hell are we all doing here?" he asked me. "Loch?"

I shrugged. "Hell if I know."

. . .

"Did you do something?" Arthur asked.

"What would I do?" I replied. "I'm a good boy."

Van laughed and nearly tumbled his chair backward.

I grinned. "What? I am."

"You didn't get someone pregnant, did you?" Van asked.

I pointed at him. "Hey, you watch your mouth," I said, before mumbling, "I sure as hell fucking hope not…"

"Shh." Christophe held up his hand. "Van, sit properly, will you? Get your feet off the table."

Van rolled his eyes and mouthed, "okay, *dad*."

"What is this, Christophe?" I asked him. "Do you have any idea?"

"No, I told you, I don't know. Mother and Father didn't say."

. . .

As if on cue, the dining room doors swung open again, and our parents entered. The four of us quickly rose to our feet. Van caught my eye and gave me a little wink. I grinned and winked back at him before taking a serious expression to address our parents. "Good morning, Mom. Good morning, Dad."

Dad's face was as stern as always. My brothers and I (minus Christophe, who had taken Dad's seriousness) always used to joke that Dad's constant scowl was where the Crescent Moon Clan got its name. I resisted the urge to crack a grin thinking about it.

"Mm," he grunted. "Good morning, son."

For a moment, I wondered if they were going to scold me for having spent the night out without giving any notice, but Mom turned to Van and told him that he needed to comb his hair.

"Sit down, all of you," Dad said, his voice a stiff growl. We did as we were told.

My parents took seats at the opposite end of the table, facing me. Our dusty old dining room table was unnecessarily long, and it felt like they were a mile away. I sat silently, waiting for them to say what this was all about. All four of us were looking at them.

. . .

Dad folded his hands on the table and spoke with a voice that sounded like he was addressing the entire clan. "I've spent the past three days meeting with Julius and Desmond Croc in regards to the peace between our two clans."

The Ice River Pack. In my grandfather's time, it was customary to spit on the floor whenever their name was mentioned. When my father took over as leader, he put a stop to the habit after the peace pact was made between our clans. I knew that a lot of the older generation Crescent Moons still held a hate for them, but personally, I never fully understood why. The bad blood between the clans originated from some stupid disagreement from like, 200 years ago.

"As much as it stings my pride to talk about our financial predicaments, we aren't in a position to ignore the situation, as you all know."

My brothers and I all nodded our heads. If our finances were teetering on the edge, it meant a wavering in our authority and power and would put our family in a position to be challenged by one of the other Crescent Moon families, or even an outside family. Something like that would most likely end in someone getting seriously hurt, or even killed. I couldn't imagine what I'd do if anything happened to any of my family members.

Mom spoke now. "The Crocs, similarly, are in a delicate situation. We've been negotiating with them to make an arrangement between our families to tie us together."

. . .

"We already have a peace pact with them," Van said, not without a tinge of viciousness in his voice. "What could we possibly gain from those Icers?"

"Vander," Dad said, his voice stern. "I've known Desmond Croc for over thirty years. I held hate for him, believe me, your grandfather made sure of that… but when I fought and trained with Desmond, I learned just how honorable an alpha he was. If you make judgements about a person without taking the time to understand them, then you're *useless*."

"Sorry, Dad…" Van said, sinking so low in his chair I thought he might slip away under the table.

"What negotiations?" I asked. "And how do they involve me?"

"The Crocs are still one of the wealthiest families in the country," Mom said. "To unite with them would mean the security of our family."

"Desmond and Julius have a son. An omega."

"Tresten," I said. "He's at the FAS with me."

. . .

Van perked back up. "He's an omega and he's in the FAS? That's fucking *awesome*!"

"Correct," Dad said, ignoring Van. "He's also their *only* son. Desmond came to me with this proposal when he discovered that Tresten had gotten his mark."

Arthur snorted, and Christophe pushed his glasses up and leaned back in his chair. I frowned. Apparently, they'd realized something I hadn't.

"Okay. What proposal?"

"Yeah," Van piped in. "What proposal?" He was touching his hair where his mark would show in a few years.

Christophe looked at me over the rim of his glasses. "Seriously, Loch? You're not that slow, are you?"

"What? Don't be a jerk, not everyone went to the *Leadership Arts School* like you two smartasses." I waggled my fingers in the air.

Dad's voice cut over us. "Loch."

I straightened. "Yes, Dad."

. . .

"It's been agreed upon that you and Tresten Croc will be married, in order to bind our families and our clans together."

I leapt to my feet, sending the chair bouncing back across the floor. "What?!"

"Wasn't it obvious…?" I heard Christophe mutter to Arthur. Normally I would've said something smart to him, but right now I was too fucking bewildered to do anything but stand there and try and collect my jaw from the floor.

"The Crocs have arranged a house for you two to move into after the union, and—"

"H-hold on! Dad! Mom! Wait a *second*. I am *not* getting married, especially not to Tresten Croc! A forced marriage? This is ridiculous."

I looked to my brothers for help. Christophe, of course, was straight faced and serious. Arthur looked like he was going to laugh. Vander, who I would've thought would be the one cracking up on the floor, looked freaked out and was obviously coming to grips with the fact that *he* could be the next one to be married off to someone.

. . .

Married. What the *fuck*?

"It's decided," Mom said evenly, her lips a thin line.

"It's not decided," I said. "I should have some say in this, right? It's my life. Besides, I'm in the FAS. I don't have time for that kind of shit!"

Mom flinched, and I realized I'd made a terrible mistake—I'd not only cursed in front of her, I'd talked back. I was 22 years old, but she still had no tolerance for any of that, and I prepared for her bite. She looked like she was about to explode on me, when Dad put his hand up. The room fell completely quiet and the energy that smoldered in the air faded.

"Tresten," he said.

"Dad," I replied, staring angrily down at the table with my teeth clenched. I thought of Master Graffer's lessons about presence in the moment, trying my hardest to maintain calm.

"Where does a wolf of honor, strength, and pride tread?"

Just like that, the tension disappeared from my body. I stood straight and looked into his eyes.

. . .

"Beneath the Crescent Moon," I replied.

He nodded, his chin slowly dipping once. "I know you understand what's at stake here. And that I wouldn't be asking this of you if it weren't for the strength of our family, and to preserve our position in this clan. A position we've held for *400* years."

I took a deep breath, collected my chair, and sat down. I did understand. It certainly didn't make me like what had been so suddenly thrust on me, but it did make it easier to accept. *This was happening. I had to do it.* "Yes."

"Good. Then we'll complete the arrangements to hold a legal ceremony."

Dad continued to talk, but his voice was distant while my mind filled with a whirlwind of thoughts. My life as I knew it was over. I was going to be married. And to who? Fucking Tresten Croc, the stuck-up omega with something to prove. He was cold and standoffish, and given he was an Ice River Pack member, I wouldn't be surprised if ice water was pumping through his heart.

After my parents dismissed us, I retreated to my room to contemplate my fate. I felt numb about it. The reality probably hadn't completely struck me yet. But I couldn't be angry. I was upset, but not angry. I fully understood the reason for this arrangement.

. . .

Besides, this whole thing was just for the title and clan politics. We'd be married in name, but that was it. It wasn't like I would be living with him, or sleeping with him. We'd see each other more often—I could deal with that. In the end, this would be a bump in my life and things would be basically back to normal. Word would spread at school of course, but that was fine.

And maybe, by doing this, I could finally prove to my parents that I could honor my family just as much as my brothers did.

TRESTEN

After my parents informed me that I was soon to be Loch Luna's omega groom, I excused myself to go outside. In a daze, I walked through the apple orchard that was behind the house towards the private area I used as a training ground. The call of crickets filled the night air, and the moon shone brightly in the sky, casting shadows against the apple trees.

Pa and Dad reassured me that I would not have to withdraw from the Dawn Academy—a relief, because *that* I would've fought against—but still, to be training at the FAS while *married* to one of the other alphas? It would be… horrendous. I couldn't imagine the shit we would both get from everyone in the school.

Loch was a stranger. How could I marry someone I hardly even knew? I didn't hate him, but Loch was… ugh.

. . .

I saw a memory of him in the hallway at the Fighting Arts School, propping himself up with one hand while he sat midair in a lotus position. He was shirtless, and had shifted to let his tail bush out behind him. I remembered how a pair of alpha females getting out of a lesson walked by him, and how he gave them the dumbest smile.

The guy was a playboy and a joke. He was a strong fighter but he never seemed to take things completely seriously. It pissed me off that he was just sailing by on his natural talents, while some people like me were working their asses off to be the best.

The trees opened up into a circular dirt clearing that was my training area. I walked to the center and dropped onto my back. Even though the moon glowed brightly, the sky still shimmered with stars. I breathed in the comforting smell of the apple trees and closed my eyes. Suddenly, it felt like a great pit had bottomed out inside me, emptying out everything good and happy that I felt.

This was going to be the rest of my life.

With my focus on training, I'd hardly given it thought before, but I did want a partner eventually. In a few years, it would've been nice to find someone to fall in love with. Someone I *really* wanted to marry. Yeah, I would've liked that. I would've wanted to start a family.

. . .

That pit inside me widened, and I felt a deep ache that I'd never felt before. All sorts of thoughts and ideas rushed through my mind. A child from a love I would now never meet. That man's unknown face, and all the experiences of love that would never happen. A happy family.

A thought of Loch flashed through my mind again. I saw his body, hardened and strong, and his red alpha eyes gazing directly into mine. I felt an electric surge of excitement pulse down to between my legs. My heart jumped.

Shocked, I sat up and punched the dirt. *What the hell was that?*

The thoughts of mating, of having a child... I'd never felt this way before. And even remotely considering Loch as being attractive? My heart pounded. Was it because of the mark? Because I was in heat?

It didn't matter, because there was no way I would fall in love with someone like Loch Luna.

* * *

"I'm not joking," I said, and the laughter that had been ringing through my cellphone was swallowed into a beat of stunned silence. Unable to fall asleep, I'd called Velvy to break the news to her.

. . .

"Your parents can't expect you to actually go through with it," she said.

"Velvy, come on. You're the history student."

"I know. I mean, I've read about arranged marriages between the high-born families, but just… it seemed so far away. Even after coming to Dawn Academy, and having you as a friend. It's still unreal to someone like me."

"I know."

"And it's tradition that they made all the arrangements without you even knowing?"

"Yeah."

"I can't even imagine how you must be feeling right now, Tresten. I'm sorry."

Sighing, I laid back onto my bed and stared at the ceiling. Above my bed, there was a series of grooves and bumps in the stucco that seemed to form either a wolf, an airplane, or a face, depending on how you looked at it. Such a simple thing had been a part of nearly my entire life, there every single night I went to bed.

. . .

"It's strange," I said, "to think that I'm going to be moving out of my house in a couple days. Being uprooted on such short notice... so strange. Moving in with... him. Getting *married* to him. This was not how I thought my life was going to be like, not at all."

"What is he like?"

"A fool," I said instantly.

"Why is he a fool?"

I brushed my hair out of my face. "He's the type of alpha who loves to put on a show just to try to get attention. He's more muscle and brawn than anything else. I mean, he's two years older than I am, and even after an extra two years of training he *still* relies on his muscles to fight, not realizing the brain is just as important. How can you win a fight if you're not thinking and paying attention? He goes completely by his intuition, which is often just plain wrong. I also hate the way he always bugs me whenever he sees me in the hallways, like he hasn't gotten the hint that I don't care to be friendly with him. Not to mention, how he *loves* to shift his ears and tail out to look like some ridiculous puppy-boy, just so he can thrive on the reaction the girls get when they see him. It's *not* cute, it's *not* adorable, it's just stupid."

"Wow. It sure sounds like you pay a lot of attention to him."

. . .

Velvy sounded amused, and I flushed. "No, fuck, no. He's just been around in my life for a very long time. I pay as little attention to him as possible."

"Mm. I dunno, Tresten. It sounds like you're being a little harsh, don't you think? You've always seemed to dislike perfectly nice guys. It's why you've never dated."

"I've never dated because I have no time for it," I said. "Studying and training all the time. No time, no energy. Plus, it would dull my skills."

"Go into it with an open mind," she said. "Maybe you'll find you two are actually good for each other? You mentioned he's always tried to be friendly? Come on, Tresten! Don't be a jerk. I know you told me that you wanted to try and be nicer to people, right?"

"Yeah, but not him. Look, it's not exactly easy for an omega in the Fighting Arts School. Most of the alphas there dislike me. It's easier to just ignore them all and focus on my own training. I've become strong by doing that. I'm not distracted by—"

"—How sexy they are?"

"…No."

. . .

Velvy broke into a fit of laughter. "I'm just saying to go in with an open mind. He's been friendly, so maybe he'll be open to the whole thing too. That's all I'm saying. It's better than fighting against it and making it hard for yourself."

I sighed. "I'm getting *married* to this guy, Velvy. This isn't just a temporary thing. I can't back out if things don't work. How can I be expected to be married to someone I feel nothing for?"

I remembered that excited rush I'd gotten when I was in my training area, and pushed the feeling away. *I'm not attracted to this guy. Not one bit.*

* * *

The next day was a Saturday, and my parents and I were chauffeured to the Grand Circle, the big hall downtown where the leaders of the most powerful clans came to meet, and where legal proceedings were held. We drove between the gigantic stone wolf statues of the city's ancient founders that stood astride the entrance to the hall grounds, and the road veered right in a giant half circle around the front courtyard. In the courtyard was another massive statue, this one of a man standing side by side with a wolf. The man held an open book in his hand, and the wolf a sword between his jaws. In the distance, the structure that was the Grand Circle lay like an enormous stone ring turned on its side. It'd always made me think of a prison collar.

. . .

Pa was talking into his cell phone. "Fantastic. Make the arrangements to purchase all the essentials they'll need. I want only the best for them. You know I do. Good. Okay. Thank you. I will. Goodbye." He slipped the phone into his breast pocket. "Well, that's that," he announced. "The home is ours—yours, I mean. You will move in together after the ceremony."

I stared out the window at the Grand Circle growing closer and larger. It was four stories high and had been built around the time of the Dawn Academy. I adjusted the big bow collar of the traditional omega dress robe my parents had insisted I wear to the ceremony. I felt ridiculous, like I was a present to be unwrapped. It was all froofy and ornamental and completely the opposite of the usual easy athletic fight gear I liked to wear. "It's all so fast," I said. "Is it really necessary that he and I live together?"

"Of course," said Pa. "We have an image to uphold as the leaders of our clan. You two will need to have a child to solidify our pact, and that can't happen if you both are in different houses, isn't that right?"

I shuddered. "Please don't talk about children, Pa. I might throw up."

"I know it's difficult," Dad said gently. "This is a situation we would never have put you in if it were not of such importance."

. . .

I wasn't angry with my fathers. I knew my duty. I was just still having a hard time coming to terms with the reality of the whole situation.

"This is a trial, Tresten," Pa said, his voice firm and commanding. I turned away from the window to look at him and saw a shimmering of fire in the back of his red alpha eyes. Everything left my mind; my attention was completely his. "This is a trial more difficult than any matchup, or exercise, or test the alphas at the Fighting Arts School could put you through. This is *your* trial. It is a life trial. It has no end, and will continue to test you and push you every day. Do not let yourself become disheartened, and do not allow yourself to be broken. I don't know what kind of man Loch Luna is. Men may change their face once behind the doors of their own home. If he turns out to be a dishonorable alpha, you cannot let him defeat you. Fulfill your duty, but do not let him defeat you. Do you understand me, Tresten?"

I felt a well of energy inside me. *This is my trial.* I hadn't thought about it that way before. "Yes, Pa," I said. "I understand."

He nodded. "Good. You're a capable wolf, Tresten. I know just how strong you are. You *are* my son, after all. You're our son."

My heart filled with pride hearing those words from him. I would not fail my clan.

. . .

The Grand Circle was bustling with a mix of workers, clan officials, and ordinary people there to settle legal matters, disputes, and unions. When the limousine pulled around to the front, two large alpha males in black suits arrived to chaperone us into the building. Along the way, we had to stop several times to greet people—allies of our clan, businessmen, and well-wishers.

"You must be Master Tresten Croc," an older alpha with a storm of grey hair said to me after greeting my fathers. "My name is Marten Uriel. Your father had just graduated the Fighting Arts School when I started my first year. There were still whispers of his name around the hallways, even when he was gone. He's a legend."

"Hardly," Pa said.

Dad stood next to him, his arm through his. "He was a legend in the Healing Arts School, as well. Legendary for injuring himself in the most ridiculous ways."

"Himself, and others," Marten said, and both he and Pa laughed heartily.

My fathers and I continued on, still flanked by the two alpha bodyguards, until we reached an elevator with golden doors carved with an intricate relief of the shifter historical mythology. This was the elevator which lead up to the official chambers and to my fate. He was waiting up there for me —my *fiancé*. I felt a sudden urge to turn around and run, to shift into my wolf form and escape. I quickly suppressed it. There would be no running. Not today, not ever. I would fight this battle head on.

LOCH

I eyed the window at the end of the conference room and strummed my fingers on the long wooden table. I could make a charge for it, shift, and blast through the thing. We were only what, four stories up? No problem. I'd be on the ground and out of here in a flash. I could leave this city and strike up a new life out in the mountains somewhere. Hell, I could train with the bear shifters.

Except I'd never do that. I would never leave my clan in a time of need, no matter what the reason was.

I continued to tap my fingers until Mom put her hand on the back of mine.

"Please stop that, Loch," she said. "It's giving me a headache."

. . .

Dad sat on Mom's other side, and his eyes were closed. He wasn't sleeping—I knew that sometimes he liked to meditate before important events. It was something he'd learned at the Fighting Arts School. I'd been taught it too, but I was too damn nervous to meditate right now. A robed officiant sat across from us, completely silent with his hands folded on the table. I squirmed. That window did seem mighty tempting.

Where were they? Maybe Tresten had convinced his parents that this was a terrible idea, and he wouldn't show. Then I wouldn't have to go through with this marriage.

It felt like my brain was tying itself into terrible knots. No matter how much I hated this, and how badly I didn't want it to happen, I didn't actually want Tresten to not show. Him not showing would mean a collapse in relations with our clans. And without the future financial support of the Crocs, my family's position would be threatened. It could mean bloodshed.

I wanted to get this all over and done with as soon as possible. Sign the paperwork, enter our names in the clan registry, *bam*, alpha and omega bonded together for life. And then I could move on with mine. I'd never be able to get married for real, but that was fine with me. I was a fighter. There was no time for things like falling in love. If I had to live a life of one night stands and bachelorhood, that was fine with me. The warrior's way was all I needed. Maybe once I knew my family was secure, I would go off to the woods after all. Training under a pounding, icy waterfall with the bear masters didn't sound so bad.

The doors to the chamber unlatched and made my heart jump a billion feet. Two men in suits entered and took both sides of the door way, and in walked Julius and Desmond Croc. I felt my mom slap my shoulder, and I realized that my parents and the officiant were all standing. I quickly pushed my chair back, causing it to honk loudly against the floor, and stood up. Then Tresten entered behind his fathers. My mouth dropped for a split second before I managed to get control over it. He was dressed up in the traditional robe, the special one that omegas wore for a small number of formal events, weddings being the main one. I admit, I'd always loved the way traditional omega robes looked on a man. It was gorgeous and accentuated his physique in all the right places, and the bow in the front made him look… surprisingly adorable.

I was shocked at myself for feeling that way about Tresten Croc. He still wore his usual cold I-hate-you expression, but somehow it'd been softened by the robe. His blue eyes met mine, and he frowned and quickly looked away. His look might've been softened, but he still was the same old Tresten.

My parents and I exchanged greetings, but Tresten and I didn't say a word to each other. We all took our seats, with him next to me and his parents to his left, and the officiant opened up a folder of documents and spread them out onto the table. I wasn't listening to anything that was being said. I just wanted to take a peek over at Tresten. I was so used to seeing him in training mode: covered in sweat and dirty, wearing a battle robe, eyes filled with rage…

"…and this marriage will join the Luna family and Croc family through the bonds of blood," the officiant said, pushing his gold wire framed glasses up his nose. "The final tie being the production of an alpha child who will represent the coupling of the two packs, and the future heir of the Ice River Pack. Is this all correct and good?"

Whoah, whoah, wait a second.

"Well and good," my parents said.

"Well and good," said Tresten's parents.

"Well and good," Tresten muttered. I looked over at him, shocked. He looked back at me and raised an eyebrow.

"Wait, wait, wait," I said, waving my hands. The officiant's glasses slid down his nose, and he pushed them up again with his thumb. I felt my parents' hot glare on me. "Child? Heir? What?"

The officiant slid his finger across the paper in front of him. "These are the terms negotiated by your parents. You both will have time to finish your studies before you conceive an heir."

"That's not happening," I said, shaking my head. Tresten was still staring me like I was crazy. How the hell was he not protesting this? "Tresten? Come on. Marriage in contract is one thing, but a kid?"

"How did you think this worked?" he said miserably.

"Loch," Mom said, her voice strained. "This arrangement includes all the expectations which come with marriage. I thought you understood that?"

"I understood this was going to be an on-paper type arrangement. Maybe take some photos, make an announcement, not an *actual* marriage."

Tresten pushed his face into his palm. "You're an idiot."

"And you're okay with this, Tresten?"

He straightened. "As long as my family is in jeopardy, I'll do what I need to, no matter how I feel about it." His words didn't match his tone. I could tell he was disgusted with the idea.

. . .

I slumped in my chair. I was in the exact same position. My family needed me, and for once, I had something that only *I* could do. "Well and good," I grunted at the table. "Next you'll be telling me we need to *live* together."

Silence.

I looked up, and the officiant's glasses slipped down yet again. He cleared his throat. "Well, actually, yes. The next stipulation on the contract is that the wedded couple will move into a home gifted by the Croc family and Ice River Pack."

"Shit."

"*Loch*," Mom hissed, and Dad gave me a sharp glare. I kept my mouth shut.

That was that.

Not only was I getting married to Tresten Croc, we were now expected to have a baby together. Fucking insane.

The officiant cleared his throat again and shuffled through the papers on the table. "Now, before we have you sign the official documents, would you like to go through the traditional marriage vows?

. . .

The two of us spoke at the same time. "No." If it were any other time, I would've laughed.

Both our parents said nothing, and I silently thanked them for at least giving us that dignity.

The officiant nodded. "Then leave your signatures here, and a paw stamp at the bottom." He pushed a long document across the table to us, which was filled with lines of delicate script-work. I took the pen, and with a deep breath reluctantly scribbled my signature onto the bottom. Tresten did the same. The officiant took the paper from the table and then set it onto a wooden tablet on the floor, and laid an inkpad next to it. Tresten and I both shifted into our wolf forms, and I couldn't help but take a moment to notice how his robe looked on his wolf. As out of place as it might've been for Tresten to be wearing an omega wedding robe, it really did look good on him.

I tamped my paw onto the ink pad and then hovered above the paper for a moment. *This is it. No turning back now. The window is still right there, you could break through it and be out of here.*

I made my print, and Tresten followed suit. We shifted back, and the officiant handed us both wet towels to clean the ink off our palms. I glanced over at my new husband. He stared ahead, his blue eyes distant.

"You are now a mated pair," the officiant announced. "Bonded in marriage. Congratulations."

* * *

The Crocs hadn't spared much expense with our new home, and seeing the grounds actually made me believe there was a silver lining to all of this craziness. It was located on the outskirts of the city on Ice River land, not too far from Tresten's family home, and was bordered by a large evergreen forest. The house itself was huge, with five bedrooms and a full training studio that had been fully equipped with all the same gear we had available at school. Out in the back there was a full-sized dirt combat circle.

Tresten and I stood at the front of the house and watched as our parents pulled away, leaving us alone together for the first time. I opened my mouth to say something, and then heard the front door open and close behind me. I turned around, and saw that he'd already gone inside.

During the ceremony, some extremely efficient movers had packed all of our things in boxes and moved them into the main room of the house, and Tresten was already in the process of lugging his boxes into one of the bedrooms.

"My Pa bought this place because the layout is split up so we can both have our own space," he said. He'd tossed the traditional robe onto the floor and had pulled on a pair of loose sweatpants. He was shirtless. "By all rights, we shouldn't ever have to see each other except for in the kitchen. I'll take the rooms on the left side of the house. Both are the same size. We can both have a study room, and the fifth room is a guest room. Is that fine?"

I put my hands up. "No complaints here. Less face time the better."

"Good."

So much for any extra softness. I grabbed the first of my boxes and lugged it to my bedroom. Like the house, my room was huge, at least three times bigger than my already spacious room at my family home. Life might not be so bad here—if I didn't have Tresten as my roommate.

No, he was my *husband*. I had to remind myself to think of him that way, because there was an image to uphold. Eyes would be on us. I could care less about my own image, but I had my family name to protect.

Which also meant… No more hookups.

Could I manage that?

For now, sure. But for the rest of my life?

. . .

"Look, Tresten," I said when we both came back to the main room to grab another box. He had broken out in a fine sweat that made his skin shimmer, and for some stupid reason, my eye was drawn to his chest. *Not anything you haven't ignored dozens of times before*. When he crouched down to wrap his arms around the box, I caught a whiff of his scent in the air. Something about it smelled different than usual.

He ignored me and hauled the box to his room. "Tresten," I said again when he returned. "We probably should talk."

"I'm not really in the mood to talk right now, Loch."

I sighed and moved a few of my own boxes to my room. "There's logistics we need to work out," I shouted.

His voice shot back across the length of the house. "You stay on your side, I stay on mine."

I walked back outside. Tresten was hoisting up the last of his boxes. "Our parents don't *actually* expect us to have children," I said, half asking and half stating hopefully. "That would just be fucking ridiculous. There's no legitimate reason for it. Our families are already bound by legal contract."

. . .

Without giving me a response, Tresten lugged the last box back to his room. What the hell was his problem? I grunted and followed after him. "Hey," I said. "Look, we might as well talk to each other—"

He threw the box halfway across his room and it exploded onto the floor, sending its contents flying everywhere. He spun around, his blue eyes piercing and cold. "I don't want to talk with you, Loch. Okay? Please, leave me alone."

He shut the door right in my face. "Fuck you too, then," I muttered.

I didn't have many things, so I left the boxes unpacked in my room and walked around the house. It was sparsely decorated, but the Crocs had purchased furniture and stocked the kitchen. I checked the fridge and was surprised to find it full of fresh ingredients. I took note of what was there and decided on what I would cook for my meal that night, and for school the next day.

My parents had someone to prepare meals, but I found he didn't cook to specifications that I'd researched and measured for my training, and so I'd taught myself how to make my own food.

I walked aimlessly around the house for a while, wondering if Tresten was going to come out of his room. Seriously, what the hell was his problem? I knew he disliked me, but I also knew he was resilient and strategic, and so I was surprised that he wasn't working with me to solve the problem we had on our hands. Why was he being so difficult?

The two rooms that I guessed were meant to be studies were empty, but the fifth room was obviously the master bedroom, and, judging from the king-sized bed, had been intended for both of us to share. Tresten must've made the decision that we were going to take the actual guest bedrooms so that we didn't have to be around each other. I wasn't complaining.

After deciding there was nothing to do and that Tresten wasn't coming out, I went down to the basement where the training room was. I flicked the light switch and the fluorescent bulbs popped on in succession, illuminating the room from one end to the other. I smiled. A well-stocked kitchen and training room were all I needed.

I tossed my shirt aside. If this place was going to be my prison, then I'd at least make the most of it. This was the start of a very long journey.

TRESTEN

I sat on the edge of my new bed and stared blankly at the sea of moving boxes scattered around my room. The one I'd thrown lay on its side, with its contents strewn across the floor. I went over to it and picked up a book from the floor. It was a copy of *How to Run with the Pack: Making Friends and Developing Relationships*. Velvy had given it to me last year for my birthday, after I'd told her that I wanted to try to be nicer to people. I'd never been one to make friends easily. She was my only friend, really.

I cracked it open to where I'd marked one of the pages and skimmed the lines.

"Remember that no matter how good a wolf's intuition is, they cannot read your mind nor can they fully understand what you feel inside. Communicating your feelings is a key component in developing a healthy friendship."

. . .

I grunted and tossed the book aside.

What did Loch know about my feelings? His idiotic question about whether our parents' expectations of us having a child were serious had pissed me off. He obviously had no clue what was at stake for my family. Of course they were serious. How could he not realize that?

This is my trial. My battle.

We'd only been under the same roof for an hour, and I was shocked to feel my armor cracking. It'd been easy to act brave and tough about the whole thing before, and I'd even felt proud of myself for dealing with the sudden news as well as I did. It'd felt like my training was working, like my mental strength had kept me from being shaken by this drastic turn in my life, but now that I was actually in the thick of it, I felt myself coming apart.

We were married. We'd likely live the rest of our lives together here. I'd have to bear his children…

I collapsed onto my knees. There was a twisting sensation in my chest, like my heart was being wrenched in two directions. I clutched my hand to my bare chest. Pa was right—this would be more difficult than anything I'd faced before, but I'd vastly underestimated just how difficult it would be.

. . .

I laid out on the floor, unable to will myself to move or get up. I watched the square of sunlight shining in through the window trace its way across the floor and up the wall.

Loch was right, of course. We did need to talk about all this. I just didn't want to confront my feelings about it. I felt like speaking to him would only make it all more real, and I didn't want that. Not at all.

I found my phone and dialed Velvy's number.

"Ding dong, are those wedding bells I hear?"

"Quiet, you," I sighed. "Well, it's done. I'm a married man and all moved in."

"That was quick."

"I know."

"How did it go?"

"My parents requested I wear the traditional omega mating robe. I felt like a complete idiot sitting there in that thing. Everyone else was wearing regular suits."

. . .

"Did you guys kiss?"

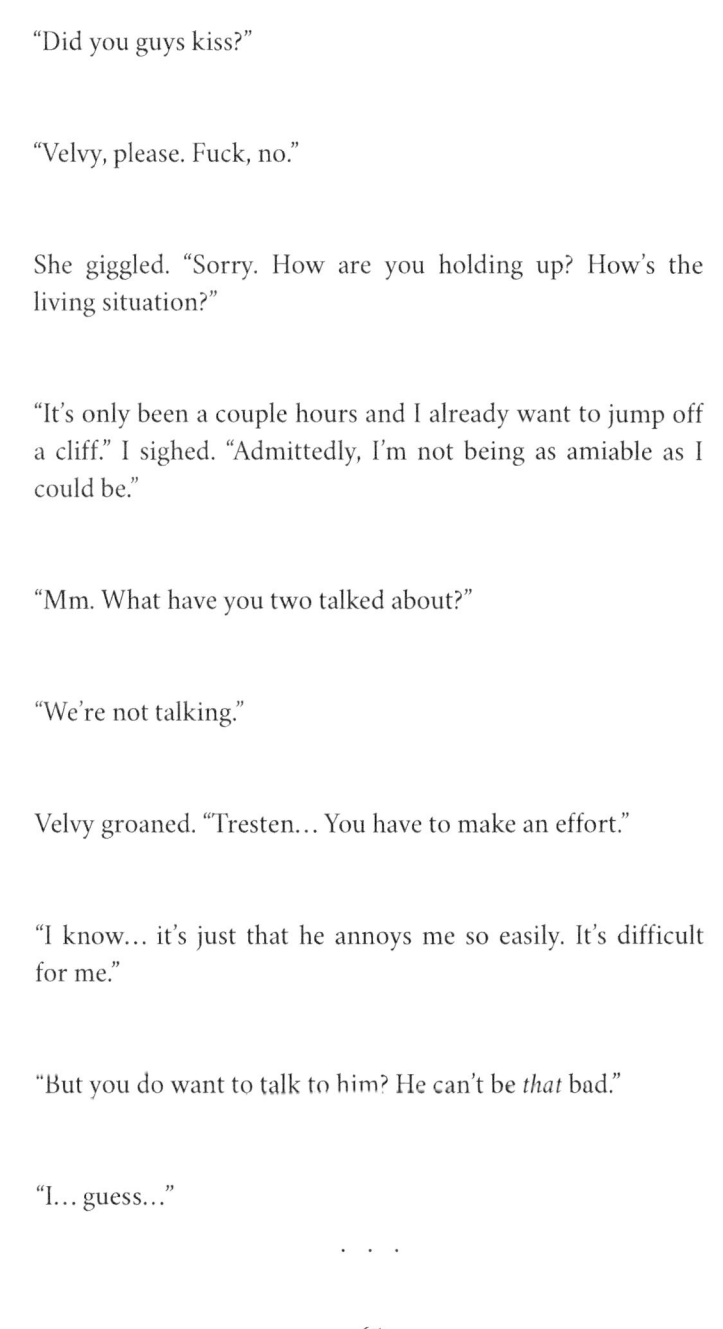

"Velvy, please. Fuck, no."

She giggled. "Sorry. How are you holding up? How's the living situation?"

"It's only been a couple hours and I already want to jump off a cliff." I sighed. "Admittedly, I'm not being as amiable as I could be."

"Mm. What have you two talked about?"

"We're not talking."

Velvy groaned. "Tresten… You have to make an effort."

"I know… it's just that he annoys me so easily. It's difficult for me."

"But you do want to talk to him? He can't be *that* bad."

"I… guess…"

. . .

"Okay, then. Try and understand where he's coming from. He might a dumb alpha, but I'm sure there's more to him than that. Just try listening to what he has to say. Be calm about it."

"Mm. Thanks, Velvy. I'll try."

We chatted for a little while longer, until she announced that she had a date to go on. "Apparently, you can meet guys in the library after all," she said. "He's a beta, too. Architecture studies. He's super cute."

"Maybe you should marry him," I said.

"Bye, Tresten," she laughed. "Remember, see where he's coming from."

I stayed on the floor of my room, and watched as the sunlight shimmering against the wall went from a pale yellow to a rich orange. It was becoming evening, and I'd been laying in my room for nearly five hours.

Enough, already.

I sat up and took a deep breath, then let it out. I searched through the boxes and found a shirt, and then slowly opened my bedroom door and peeked my head out. It was silent, and the hall was dark. I made my way out into the main room, flicking on the lights. Was he in his room?

The door was open, and his room was dark. His moving boxes were stacked up next to the bed, untouched and unpacked. Nobody there. I left the room and walked around the house, both looking for him and familiarizing myself with my new home. The place was so huge and empty, and didn't feel much like a home at all.

I passed the kitchen and felt my stomach rumble. What was I going to eat? I realized that my parents hadn't hired any help for us. I was so used to William preparing meals for me back home. Cooking—another new challenge to conquer. I checked the fridge and found that it was filled with raw ingredients. I picked up a pack of thick, red beef steaks and examined them.

Well, if all else failed I could just shift into wolf form and eat the meat raw…

I shuddered at the thought.

Where was Loch? He wasn't in any of the other rooms. I walked down the stairs leading to the basement training room, and paused at the door. There was muffled music thumping from the other side, and when I cracked the door I got a face full of blaring rock music.

. . .

Loch stood at the center of the room, stripped down to his underwear, his body glistening with sweat, and his hair and wet. Up on the wall was a digital timer, the automatic kind that could be used to track shifting speed. He let out a loud roar as he dashed forward, and his body shifted rapidly into his wolf form. The timer's counter flashed through the numbers until he completed the shift, and it froze with a loud buzz. He looked up at it and barked an annoyed growl, and then shifted back to human. The timer reset.

I watched him silently from the doorway as he shifted again and again, trying to make a dent in his time. Had he been doing this for the whole time I was in my room? Judging from how worn down he looked, I wouldn't have been surprised.

Ugh. I couldn't bear to watch anymore of this torture.

"You'll burn yourself out, doing that," I shouted over the blaring sound of guitar. Loch turned around, his red eyes glinting under the fluorescent ceiling lights. He went over to the wall, where his clothes were tossed onto the ground, and picked up a towel and his cell phone. He touched the screen, and the music turned off.

"Your parents really hooked it up," he said. "We've got top of the line stuff here. Great sound system too."

. . .

I felt a tinge of irritation that Loch was using things provided by my parents. We had the best because my fathers wanted the best for me, not for some freeloader.

Patience, keep it in check.

I took a deep breath and reminded myself that this was an even trade and that Loch was helping my family, even if he didn't know it or particularly care. *Not only that, but this whole thing affects him just as much as it does you. It's his life too, remember.* The hot annoyance slowly simmered down.

Loch dried his chest off with his towel. "Done moping around?" he asked.

I felt my face go hot. So much for simmering down.

"I was not moping around," I said.

"It seemed like you were moping."

"I wasn't. I was just upset."

"So, moping then."

. . .

I balled my hands into fists, and tried to remember the calmness exercises from training. "I… apologize for my behavior," I muttered.

Loch slipped back into his t-shirt and jeans. "Thanks," he said before flipping the lights off and walking past me and out of the training room.

"Hey," I said, following after him up the stairs. He tossed his towel onto the back of the couch and then went to the kitchen and started to rummage through the fridge.

He looked over at me. "What happened to seeing each other as little as possible?"

I flushed again. "Weren't you the one who said we should talk?"

"Changed my mind." He tossed a pack of steak onto the counter, along with a head of broccoli, a fat carrot, and an onion. "I think things will be more pleasant for me if I just leave you be."

"Alright, fine," I grunted, and stormed back to my room. I slammed the door behind me and plonked myself onto the bed. If he wanted to be difficult then I had no problem with being difficult. Difficult was my natural state.

. . .

A short while later I caught the rich aroma of grilled meat drifting underneath my door. My stomach roared. I hadn't eaten anything since morning. When I went out to the kitchen again, Loch was standing in front of the stove monitoring a sizzling slab of steak.

Dammit, it smells so good.

I quietly went to the fridge and pulled out one of the other packs of raw steak and set it onto the counter. After finding a pan, I cut open the package and set the pan onto the stove next to Loch's. I snuck a glance over at his. Did he just turn the heat on and slap it onto the pan? I honestly had no idea what to do.

After examining the buttons on the front of the stove, I figured out how to activate the damn thing and turned the heat on. I snuck another side glance, and set it to the same setting as Loch's. Then I got the meat and dumped it into the pan.

Loch snorted.

"What?" I demanded, feeling my face go red.

"You might want to use some oil," he said. "And it would help if the pan was hot."

. . .

I frowned and started to look through the cabinets.

"Here." He held out a bottle of cooking oil.

"Thanks," I grunted, taking it. I used a spatula to lift the meat off the pan, and then poured out the oil.

"Are you trying to drown the poor thing?"

"No," I said. "Leave me alone. I can take care of it myself."

I set the meat back in the pan, and yelled when the oil splattered up and scalded my arm. Loch pushed me out of the way and turned off the burner. "You're going to burn our brand-new house down," he said. "You've never cooked before, have you?"

I took a step back, feeling embarrassed and useless. "Watch how I do it," he said, taking the pan off the stove and dumping the oil into a glass. He then twisted the salt and pepper shakers on both sides of the meat before returning it to the range. After a moment, the meat started to sizzle. "You put way too much oil. Just a tiny bit. Enough to coat the pan. Got it?"

I nodded. "Yeah…"

. . .

He held up six fingers. "Six minutes. Flip it every minute. Don't press the steak. And don't put the heat too high." He flipped his steak over and then held the spatula out to me. "Okay?"

"Thanks," I said.

"Is your arm okay?"

"It's fine. Thank you." I came back up to the stove and the two of us stood silently, staring at our pans.

"You really don't know how to cook?" he asked, after a moment.

"Well, I… no." We both flipped our steaks over.

"It's not too hard," he said. "You'll pick it up fast."

I blinked. I'd expected an insult, not encouragement.

"My family, we have a chef that cooks for us," I said. "So I'd never had to learn."

. . .

"Mine too. But he never could make food that I thought was up to my nutritional needs, so I ended up just doing it myself. Turned out, it was actually pretty fun."

"Ours was excellent," I said, thinking of William's delicious cooking. "He cooked special meals for me, for my training. Pa always made sure everything was to his standard."

We flipped our steaks again.

"Your Pa," he said. "That's… Master Desmond Croc, right?"

"That's right."

"Yeah, it's no wonder you've got the best of the best. My dad used to tell me and my brothers stories sometimes when we were younger about his days at the FAS. He always talked about your Pa. He's a legend."

I swelled with pride like I always did when someone mentioned a story about Pa. "I want to be as strong a fighter as he is," I said.

"I know," Loch said. "It's obvious. And it shows."

. . .

"Who's your idol?" I asked. Loch turned his burner off and pulled the pan off the stove.

"I don't have one," he said. "Give yours another minute. I made some steamed vegetables. Take some."

"You don't have an idol? No one you look up to?"

Loch took his plate and started to walk out of the kitchen. He paused, then turned around and set it down on the counter to eat there. "I look up to my brothers, though I also hate their guts sometimes. I look up to my parents, even though I don't know if they give much of a shit about me. I look up to all my brothers at the FAS—including you. And most of all, I look up to myself. Because I'm a badass."

I rolled my eyes and laughed. "Okay."

I turned off the burner, transferred the steak to a pan, and went to join him at the counter. After waiting a few minutes for it to cool, I cut off a piece and took a bite. It was delicious —but I was also starving and anything would've been good at that moment.

"How's your very first meal?" Loch asked, chewing on a piece of his steak.

. . .

"It feels great to eat something you made yourself," I observed.

He smiled. "Hey, this is our first dinner as a married couple. Who would've thought? You and I, married. What a nightmare."

"It really is," I said. "But it's for our families."

"That's right," he said.

We stared at our plates and finished the rest of the meal in silence. I could feel the weight of this entire arrangement looming over us, but in the end, neither one of us wanted to talk about it after all. After dinner, we both went to our rooms and shut the doors. I was exhausted from the day's events, and collapsed onto the bed.

One thought repeated in my mind for the few short moments before I drifted into sleep.

How am I going to have a baby with him?

LOCH

I was used to waking up in the morning to unfamiliar ceilings, but this one belonged to me. I blinked and rubbed my eyes, and I remembered where I was. *New home. Moved out. Got married.*

I dug through the cardboard moving boxes until I found my training bag, and got dressed in my usual athletic wear, over which I slipped my battle robe. Embroidered on the collar was the Fighting Arts School and the Dawn Academy's emblems, and I ran my finger along the stitching. After washing up in the bathroom, I went outside to cook up something to bring to school for lunch, and ran into Tresten, who was also going to the kitchen.

"Good morning," he mumbled.

. . .

"Mornin'," I mumbled back, and we both went into the kitchen and started to fumble around awkwardly, trying to stay out of each other's way. His hair was tousled from sleep, and he wore an oversized t-shirt and a pair of boxers. I knew there was no reason I should be feeling this way—after all, it was only Tresten—but it felt strangely intimate to be seeing him like this.

It's just Tresten. Guy you've known for years. Guy you've fought dozens of times, and trained with every day. Guy you don't particularly like very much.

So why did things feel… different?

I watched as Tresten pulled out a package of raw chicken and looked at it like it was the weirdest thing he'd ever seen. He brought out the pan and set it on the stove, and then stared helplessly at the chicken.

"You know what you're doing with that thing?" I asked.

"I've got it," he said sharply. After a few moments, he hung his head sheepishly and mumbled, "I don't know what I'm doing."

"How about this? I'll make our meals, and you can watch until you've gotten a hang of the whole cooking thing."

. . .

He considered this, and then nodded. "Alright."

Well, damn. He *could* be agreeable after all.

I started on the food, and he stood next to me and watched me cook.

"Do you think word will have gotten around already?" he asked. "About our arrangement, I mean."

"If it hasn't, then it won't be long," I said. "Something like this is going to get around fast. You know what we should do? Go to school separately."

"I was thinking the same thing."

"I figure, the longer we can keep this on the down low, the better. The less shit I'll need to put up with, the better…"

Tresten smirked. "Is it going to bother you that much? Whatever shit you get, I'm going to get it ten times worse."

"I can deal with it. But I know assholes like Martin Bellock won't let it go. He's the kind of guy who'll pick at any weakness you have to get an advantage."

. . .

"True. Though, it's better to confront your weaknesses rather than avoiding them."

I smiled. "Ain't nothing wrong with a bit of strategy to soften the blows." I took the chicken off the burner and transferred it onto a plate. Tresten searched around the drawers and cabinets until he found two containers we could use to hold our lunches, and I split the chicken into them with the leftover vegetables. "So, we agree? We go separately, we come back separately, we don't talk."

Tresten shrugged. "Of course. Nothing has changed. It's not like we talked before."

"Why is that, anyway?" I asked. "You know, you might have some friends if you weren't always so cold. It doesn't hurt to talk to people."

His expression had been calm, but in one moment it flashed to icy annoyance. There was no middle ground with him.

"Chew a bone," he said.

"I'm serious," I said.

. . .

"Thanks for cooking," he said. "You should leave first." He took his food, and I watched him leave the kitchen. A moment later, I heard the door of his room shut.

I chuckled. I'd thought that because of the whole cooking thing he'd be more open to talking now, but apparently not.

Still, something did feel different. Our conversation the night before, though short, was something new. It was strange, but I'd felt a little thrill of excitement when Tresten had opened up to me, even if it was just a little bit. All of a sudden I wanted to know more about him—funny, considering I couldn't have cared less about him before. I'd admired him for his strength, sure, but he'd never registered as anything more than a stuck-up brat. But now… now there was something strangely alluring about that stuck-up brat. I realized that I wanted to break through that icy armor of his and find out what was beneath.

* * *

I anticipated that our marriage was going to be on the lips of every person in the FAS, but when I came in to the training gym, there was no mention of it at all. Everyone greeted me just the same, and there were no snickers or prods and elbows. It was Martin Bellock's silence that confirmed to me that word hadn't gotten around yet.

Good. The longer, the better.

. . .

Tresten took his usual lonely spot on the opposite wall of the gym, while I chatted with the usual guys. Vern Kress had a new fight strategy video to show us, and I watched it for a while but found my eye wandering back to where Tresten was. He was stretching out his body. My attention turned fully to him now, and I watched him go through his routine.

I'd never really taken much notice of Tresten's appearance before. His body was different than just about everyone's I'd seen before. He was lean and trim, with impressive sculpting of his muscles that came from precise training—but that was only the most basic thing. The *real* difference was something much more... primal.

I couldn't believe I'd never noticed it before, but I saw it fully and plainly right now.

The real difference was that *he was an omega.*

The way his ass swelled to meet his toned thighs. The subtle but sensual way his hips were wider than an alpha or beta's. The way that mark in his hair seemed to glow like a bolt of lightning.

I swallowed.

. . .

Yeah, you would notice these things. It's normal. After all, you're an alpha, he's an omega... but it doesn't mean you're actually attracted *to him*.

Tresten squatted down and stretched out his legs. He was wearing his battle robe, and his bare thighs emerged from beneath the fabric when he leaned to grab his toes. I was surprised to feel my heart jump at the sight, and the hair on the back of my neck stand on end. *It's natural, but doesn't mean a thing.*

I looked away—and that was when I made a sudden and shocking observation.

All around the training gymnasium, there were *other alphas staring at Tresten*.

I frowned. It was a coincidence.

But no... I continued to observe, and saw that, yeah, there were at least four other alphas watching him. Tresten stood up and leaned over to touch his toes, and I saw one alpha—Jackson VanKrennick from the Timber Shadow Pack—literally lick his lips, his eyes widening slightly.

Suddenly, the image of an innocent sheep oblivious to the wolves surrounding it flashed through my mind, and I felt a strange feeling tighten around my heart.

. . .

I wanted to protect him. I didn't want a single one of those motherfuckers touching Tresten.

My eyes went back to watching him again. He seemed completely unaware that anyone was looking at him—

Right at that moment, his ice blue eyes shifted and met mine. He frowned and mouthed "what?"

Just two days ago, I would've shrugged and gone back to my business. I felt a strange and powerful tug that made me leave the group and stride over to Tresten, and I knew that the people who'd been staring at him would see.

"Hey," I said. "You want to partner up today?"

He eyed me, and I was certain he was going to tell me to chew a bone.

"Is it a good idea?" he asked.

I shrugged. "Why not? There's nothing wrong with two classmates partnering up. Maybe you can give me some speed-shift pointers."

. . .

The slightest smile cracked his lips. "You do need some pointers. I watched you—" He lowered his voice. "—last night. Trying to gain speed through repetitive shifting won't help. It'll only burn you out."

"Enlighten me, then," I said.

"It's all about this." He tapped his head. "And how you use it. So, you might be a lost cause already." His thin smile widened into a grin.

"Chew a bone," I said. "So, what do I need to do, then?"

"It's all about your mind-state. It goes back to what we were told when we first learned how to shift. Focus, clear your mind, draw out the wolf from within."

"So…"

"So, you need to be exercising your focus and removing the blocks in your mind that keep you from accessing your wolf."

"I have *no* idea what those might be," I said, laughing.

He nodded. "It's a journey. Anyway, I don't know how much my advice is worth. You were right, I have gotten slower."

. . .

"What's keeping you from your wolf?"

Tresten's eyes seemed to flash with a brief moment of conflict before he looked away from me. "I don't know," he said flatly.

The doors flew open, and Master Graffer made his usual grandiose entrance. "Gentlemen! Attack and defense drills. I'll be pairing you off today, since you mongrels never want to change up your partners. Everyone line up."

Tresten and I exchanged a glance, and we joined the rest of the class in the middle of the gym. Master Graffer fired off names, and by the end of it I was paired up with none other than dog shit for brains Martin Bellock. Tresten, by all luck, was paired with Jackson VanKrennick. I felt an odd twinge of annoyance.

I'm not jealous. I was just hoping to get some pointers today, that's all.

I also was genuinely unhappy about being paired with Martin. My family had never gotten along well with his. With their new money, they loved flaunting their status, especially when they caught wind of my family's troubles. Plus, the guy just pissed me off. He was the kind of person who'd have no problem throwing a cheap shot at you, or attacking you while your back was turned. He'd seriously injured people before, but because his father always donated huge amounts of money to the Dawn Academy, he'd never been expelled. The worst part was that he was legitimately one of the strongest, if not *the* strongest fighter in our class.

We lined up and faced off, waiting for Master Graffer to command us to shift and start the drills.

"Hey, dog shit," Martin said, his lips curling into an idiotic grin. "Ready to get your ass beat?"

"Speak for yourself," I grunted.

"Begin! Go to half-shift," Master Graffer shouted.

I reached inside and found the primal form of my wolf hiding deep in the den of my mind, and concentrated on drawing him out. *Fast. Shift fast.* Martin was still faster. I was still making the transformation when his clawed meaty fist came swinging at my face, and I just barely blocked him.

"Fucking asshole," I growled under my breath.

We exchanged blows—attack, defend, attack, defend. I managed to ward off every attack he threw at me, and

Martin was the same—but it seemed like he was barely trying.

"You know, I heard something recently." Everyone's voice became rougher and deeper when they shifted, but Martin's had always sounded like the belch of a toad. "I heard the Lunas aren't doing so hot right now. Heard you're a little short on cash."

"Is that right?" I dodged a swipe of his claws and returned with a snap of my jaws towards his open torso. "Just like the Bellocks are short on brains?"

He snorted, his yellow fangs glistening in a nasty grin. My next attack missed, and I was thrown off balance. My ears pricked up, detecting the sound of his fist whistling through the air behind me, but it was too late. Pain exploded through me as it impacted against my side and hurtled me to the ground, my snout smashing into the dirt. I sneezed and blew up a puff of brown dust. Out of the corner of my eye, I saw Tresten drilling with Jackson.

Again, I felt that bizarre twinge in my chest.

Martin laughed. "What's it like being the third alpha in the family?"

I flushed anger. *Be cool,* I thought. *Just be cool.*

. . .

"I'm surprised your parents even bothered putting you through school. What a waste of money."

Normally, I would've been cool. Things usually didn't get to me. I could take the shit talking. But now Martin was touching a very, very sore nerve. I gritted my teeth and pushed myself up off the ground. "Chew a bone, you inbred, mangy fuck. Go back to the—"

Martin didn't wait for me to stand, and lashed out with a kick right at my face. I barely dodged it, and stumbled backwards onto my ass.

"Bellock!" Master Graffer shouted. "Watch those attacks. First and last warning!"

Martin put up his hands, his lips pulled back in his ugly snarl of a grin. "Sorry, master," he said.

I was doing everything I could to keep the unexpected surge of anger from bubbling over. *How dare he*. My body was trembling, my fists balled up so tight that my claws were threatening to pierce my own flesh. I should've just let it go when it happened, because now there was blood in the water. Martin knew he'd gotten to me, and when he knew he'd gotten to people, he loved to stick his finger in the wounds.

. . .

My attacks struck air, and his struck flesh. He was toying with me now. I needed to calm myself down and think straight.

"You know," he grunted in a low voice, only loud enough for me to hear. "If your family needs money, I could do you a favor. Your little brother's an omega, right? I'd pay good money for his tight little—"

There's not much room for control when all you see is red. Protocol, honor, training—it all vanished in an instant. I wanted to kill him. I wanted to get my fangs into his neck and rip out his fucking jugular.

I charged at him, intending to do just that.

TRESTEN

I heard Loch's angry roar and turned to see him barreling down on Martin Bellock with fangs and claws bared. I immediately saw his killing intent. Whatever Martin had said to him had completely overcome his senses and made him go wild. I'd never seen him like that before.

Loch already was not a controlled fighter. He too often relied on pure strength to win, and this was a matchup where he needed to use his mind. Whatever concentration he had was completely gone, and his attacks had no effect. It was over in an instant. I watched in shock as Martin sunk his fangs into Loch's left shoulder. The entire class had stopped. Master Graffer was shouting.

No time to think. I charged, dropping to all fours as my body completed the shift to full wolf, and rammed my head against Martin's neck. He released his grip on Loch and staggered back. Loch dropped to the floor, blood pouring from his wound. I stood over him, snarling at Martin, my fur and tail all pricked to aggressive defensiveness. Master Graffer came between us.

"He attacked me," Martin said, rubbing his neck. He'd shifted back to human form. "I was defending myself."

"This lack of restraint is unacceptable. Bellock, you're dismissed."

"But, Master—"

"*Dismissed!*"

Martin left a with a smirk on his face.

"Bastard," Loch growled. I stepped away, and we both shifted back to human form. "Thanks for getting him off me, Tresten." He cringed. He had his palm pressed solidly against his wound, but blood still gushed out from underneath his hand.

"Hang in there," I said. I knew he'd be fine—but the wound seemed to be pretty bad. If Martin had landed this attack on his neck… What was it that he'd said that had caused him to lose control? Loch wasn't the most disciplined, but he wasn't the type to go off on someone like that.

. . .

"I'll be fine."

Master Graffer knelt down to inspect Loch's shoulder. "He went deep," he said. "Someone call Doctor Vectus. We've got a good training opportunity for his students here. Loch, keep pressure on that wound."

Loch nodded weakly. I reached down and pressed my hand on top of his to help him. His hot blood flowed out between his fingers and ran over my hand. He looked up at me, and I was surprised by the immense strength that flowed behind his ruby eyes. I'd never seen him this way before. He smiled at me gratefully. "Never thought you'd be worried about me," he said.

"Who said I'm worried? I'm just helping out a fellow classmate."

"Well, good. I wouldn't want you to fall in love with me or anything—ah! Ow, ow, ow!"

I pushed down on his hand a little harder than was probably necessary. "Keep that pressure on it," I said loudly

* * *

After the doctor and three of his medical students came to inspect the wound, Loch was sent home for the day for recovery. The bite had torn muscle, and he was advised to take the week off to avoid further injury. The rest of the day I found myself distracted and thinking about him.

Mostly, I was surprised by my reaction to the whole thing. Would I have acted that way if it were someone else? *Yes,* I told myself. *Definitely.*

But I wasn't convinced.

I thought about the feeling of his blood running over my fingers, and the sudden flame of defensiveness I'd felt when I'd stood over him, snarling. *Hell.* That was *not* normal behavior for just any old classmate.

I was supposed to meet Velvy in the library after class, but I gave her a call to let her know what had happened and said that I was going home to check up on him.

"That's very sweet of you," she said.

"I just want to make sure he's not dead or something," I said quickly, knowing full well how ridiculous that sounded.

. . .

"Keep me in the know," she said in a sing song voice before hanging up.

When I got home, I set my bag down and went straight to his room. He wasn't there. "Don't tell me," I muttered, and went down to the basement.

Loch was in the middle of the training room, again stripped down to nothing but his underwear. Sweat glistened on his skin, and it seemed like every single one of his muscles was strained and bulged. His left shoulder was wrapped in bandages. I'd seen him like this just yesterday, but now I was surprised to feel my heart jolt at the sight. I suddenly felt strangely nervous.

His eyes were closed, and he was balancing with a one-armed handstand. When I stepped into the room, he opened his eyes and elegantly flipped onto his feet. The timer on the wall buzzed, and I saw that he'd been holding the pose for two and a half hours.

"Shouldn't you be resting?" I asked.

"I tried. I couldn't just lay in bed knowing I was missing training."

"What the hell happened to make you go at him like that? That wasn't like you."

. . .

"I didn't know you knew me so well."

I gave him a look. "You may be brainless but I've never seen you lose your cool before. Everyone in class was talking about it. What did he say to you?"

He toweled off and grabbed his clothes. His left arm was confined to a sling, and he managed to slip into his pants using his good hand. I had an odd and disturbing realization that I wouldn't have minded seeing him stripped down for a little while longer. He removed the sling and pulled the shirt over his head, and stopped when he realized there was no way he'd be able to get his arm through. I stepped over and helped him get into his shirt.

"Thanks," he said.

"So, what did he say?"

"Just the usual Martin Bellock shit."

"Dog shit. I don't believe you would've put everything on the line for 'the usual shit.' I saw you. You were going for a killing blow. If Master Graffer had seen that…"

. . .

"Yeah, well, it's a good thing he didn't."

"Loch."

He sighed and sat down, his back up against the wall. He winced and held his arm. "He was talking down on my family. Giving me shit about being the third alpha."

That *was* the usual Martin shit. There was more to it than that. "And?"

"He'd heard about my family's financial problems. And he said…"

Loch's hands balled into angry fists as he repeated Martin's words. A storm of disgust tore through me.

"In hindsight, it was completely ridiculous of me to get so angry," he said, shaking his head. "You're right. I put a lot on the line by letting my emotions get to me."

I crouched down next to him. He wore his typical unaffected smile, but I saw that his fists were white and trembling.

"I wasn't in control. Now I get what you mean by clearing away the mental blocks. I went blind and this is what I got for it." He put his shaking fist against his shoulder. I reached out and rested my open palm on his hand. He looked at me, surprised.

I was just as surprised as he was. I hadn't even thought about what I was doing; my hand had just gone to his. I quickly pulled it back. My skin felt like it was tingling.

"You'll have a chance to pay him back for what he did," I said. "I'll help you. I'll train with you here while you're healing. And… I'll help you work on your shift speed."

He raised an eyebrow and looked at me for what felt like forever. My heart was pounding—*why did I feel so nervous?*

"I thought we weren't going to see each other at home," he said.

I felt my face flush. "I mean, if you don't want my help…"

"No, I do. Really. I have a lot of respect for your skill. A lot."

My face went even hotter, and I felt a funny tingling inside of me. It was the first time I'd received any kind of compliment about my abilities from an alpha who wasn't a teacher or my father. I was surprised at how nice it felt to hear him say that. I suppressed the grin from spreading across my face, not wanting Loch to know just how good he'd made me feel. "Thank you," I said evenly.

"And thank you for helping me today. Even if you *are* still a stuck-up brat." He grinned at me.

Normally a comment like that would've pissed me off—but it passed through me like a cool breeze. I snorted. "I am not," I said, and pushed him.

He winced. "Ow, ow."

I laughed, and got to my feet. "You're not getting any further sympathy from me. Stop exaggerating and take the pain like an alpha."

Loch laughed too, and the two of us left the training room and went back upstairs. "I'm going to go take a shower," he announced.

"I'm not helping you with that," I told him. "You're on your own there."

"It'd be a sad day if I needed your help to shower," he replied, and disappeared into his side of the house.

. . .

I went to the kitchen and pulled out a pack of steak from the fridge, paused, and then pulled out a second one.

It was odd. Only two days into this arrangement and I was actually finding it to be… not so horrid. I was doing my best to see beyond Loch's aloof attitude and the stupid showoff antics that had always annoyed me, and as terrible as it was, this whole incident with Martin had given me a glimpse into a deeper side of him. I'd known that he was the third alpha of his family—but I'd never stopped to think, or even remotely cared, about how it was affecting him.

I'd known that he had pride in his clan and family, but I had to admit that because he was the third alpha, I'd assumed that he didn't care much about what his family thought about what he did or what he accomplished—but now, I could sense it was the opposite.

What did this arrangement mean to him, then? Maybe the circumstances for our marriage meant more to him than it did to me. He was the third alpha, after all…

Suddenly, I felt much closer to Loch. We'd both been thrown into this whole thing against our will, but without protest because we wanted to help our families. We were like two sailors piloting a ship into a storm. We only had each other.

I smiled, and cut open the packs of steaks. I felt surprisingly *light*. I seasoned the meat, poured a bit of oil onto the pan, and then lit the stove. When it was hot, I placed the steaks onto the pan. This wasn't so difficult.

I set to work cutting up some fresh veggies, noting that I'd probably need to send for more food soon.

No—we'll have to go buy more.

I was still so used to having the staff at the house to do all the chores for me.

When the steak was nearly finished, Loch came out to the kitchen. He had his shirt off and had applied fresh bandages to his shoulder. I found my eyes lingering a little longer on his naked torso than I would've liked, but *damn*, I really hadn't taken notice of how incredibly built Loch was. His body was absolutely perfect. He might've seemed carefree, but Loch definitely put a lot of work into his training.

My mouth watered, and not because of the steak.

Whoah, there. Get it together.

"Smells good," he said. "Looks good, too. You learned quick."

. . .

"I made one for you," I said. "Didn't think you'd want to think about cooking with your arm like that."

He flexed it, and winced. "It's going to be a couple days before it heals enough to do anything useful. Thanks."

I plated the food and brought it out to the dining table. No counter eating today. We'd do things properly from here on out.

"Tresten, I… want to thank you. Thank you for agreeing to this whole thing."

I sat down and started to cut into my steak. "You're welcome. I have invested interest in seeing you kick Martin's ass. Plus, it probably would be helpful if you and I worked together. Seeing as how we're stuck with each other for our entire lives." I gave him a wry smile.

"Not just offering to help me with training. I mean the marriage. I know it must've been hard for you, with how focused you are on your training. I know how much your training means to you. Marriage isn't exactly something that would normally fit in the picture."

"It isn't. But I did it for my family. Not that I had much of a choice. The truth is… because I'm omega and the only son, my family is in a risky position."

. . .

He nodded thoughtfully. "Right, of course. I hadn't thought about that. Someone could try and challenge you for clan leader."

"It's part of the reason why I've worked so hard to be a fighter. It wasn't just to follow in my Pa's footsteps, though that was a big part of it. I didn't want to let my parents down. I needed to make sure my family was secure in any way I could." I paused. "You know, I've never told anyone that before."

"I can't say I was happy about this whole thing. I mean, it was pretty much the fucking opposite. I couldn't believe it. But my family really is in a bind. We've got some major financial problems, and thanks to you and your family, that's been settled now. I really owe you a lot."

"No, you don't. We're even. So, thank you, too." I smiled at him.

He laughed. "Okay. You know, I was so convinced this was going to be the most horrible thing ever. But... so far, it's not the worst."

I nodded and took a bite of my steak. It was juicy and delicious, just like how it was when Loch had made it. He looked like he wanted to say something more, but he was silent. He picked up his fork and stabbed the steak, and when he tried to use his left hand to cut it, he winced and dropped the knife.

"Hold on," I said, and went over to him. I took his knife and fork and cut his steak up into bite sized strips. I kept my eyes on his plate, but I could tell he was looking at me. "Don't get used to this," I told him.

I went back to my seat and dug back into my steak.

"Tresten, do you think…"

I looked up at him. "Hm?"

"Ah, never mind," he said, scratching his head. "It's nothing." He ate a piece of steak. "Not bad. Not bad at all."

I smiled. *There was that strange feeling again…* Was it… *affection?* Was I really feeling something for Loch Luna?

* * *

The next morning, I met Velvy before her classes, and walked with her from the library to the Hall of Historical Studies. I filled her in on the specifics about what had happened with Martin.

. . .

"That's so horrible," she said. "I can't even imagine being in an environment like that. With people who do things like that to each other. Don't you get tired of it?"

"I deal with it," I said.

"I could never be a fighter," Velvy said.

"How did your date go?"

"Terrible," she groaned. "You'll never believe what he did. We went to get drinks, right? Everything seemed to be going pretty well, until when we left the bar and he goes into his wolf form and *sticks his nose up to my butt!*"

"The fuck?"

"That's what I said. And he tells me that it's the best way for wolves to get to know each other, and that it was what the ancient shifter tribes of the northeast did. So that was that. I guess meeting guys in the library doesn't work out so well after all. I swear, Tresten, I have no luck with guys. Maybe you have it easy." She paused. "I'm sorry, that was insensitive. I know how you feel about your situation."

I shook my head. "Actually… I'm starting to wonder if…"

. . .

Her head swiveled so fast I thought it might fly off. "What?"

"I don't know. I'm doing my best to practice what you suggested, and I'm starting to see Loch in a different way. And with what happened yesterday, I really felt like I saw who he was. And, I *felt something.*"

She gasped. "Hounds of Hell! And it's only been two days! That's wonderful, Tresten!"

"All I said was that I felt something, I never said I was in *love* with him or anything. All I'm trying to say is that I made a connection with someone. That's it."

Velvy eyed me with the biggest shit-eating grin on her face. "You sure?"

"Yeah," I said. I wasn't sure if I even believed my own voice.

The walk to the Hall of Historical Studies took us through the large grassy area at the center of campus, where a lot of people came to relax between classes. A group of people were playing disc-catch, a game where one person would throw a flying disk and a group would try and catch it out of the air in their wolf forms. The grass was also a favorite place for couples, and there were quite a few lounging about and enjoying the pleasant weather.

. . .

"So, Tresten? Is he hot? You never filled me in on the juicy details."

"I don't know," I stammered.

"Come on, I know you must have an opinion."

"I admit… when I said that I'm starting to see him in a different way, I wasn't just referring to his personality."

Velvy laughed. "That's all I needed to know."

I saw her off at the entrance to the building, and then swung a right to take the pathway that lead southwest to the Fighting Arts School. I wondered what Loch was doing back at the house today. The poor guy would have to miss lessons for a week.

Why do I have the feeling that he's trying to train using his arm right now?

An image popped in my head of him doing a handstand on his bad arm, or shifting to his full wolf and smashing his shoulder when dropping down to all fours.

Idiot. He better not be.

. . .

The next thing that came into my mind was him shirtless, shiny with sweat. I imagined him doing that thing I always would see him do in the hallways at school, where he'd shift out his ears and tail. I shivered. I'd always thought he looked so ridiculous doing that, but...

Admit it. You completely think he's hot.

I groaned. How had things changed so fast? This kind of thing had never happened to me before in my entire life! I was so convinced that no alpha would ever change my feelings about mates and love, but... something *was* changing inside of me, and I couldn't deny it.

There hadn't been any repercussions against Martin for what he'd done—it had been within his rights outlined by the battle code since Loch had made the first move—and he was in class, surrounded by his usual cronies. No one said a word to me about Loch, so it seemed like the word about our situation had still managed not to reach the ears of the community.

The stares from the alpha males that I'd started to notice ever since I'd gotten my mark were only becoming more frequent now. During one of the day's exercises, Stell Lanford even had the nerve to come and tell me that I "smelled good."

. . .

"Go sniff your own ass," I told him.

My mind kept wandering back to Loch, wondering about what he was doing at that moment. I was so certain he was doing something stupid—and I wanted to be there.

The FAS had always been a sanctuary to me, but suddenly and surprisingly all I could think about was getting home so I could train with him.

LOCH

Having to stay home from class was fucking torture.

Before heading off in the morning, Tresten had warned me to not do anything stupid that would screw my arm up even more, but I couldn't just sit around doing nothing. We had the training yard out behind the house that had been constructed to the same dimensions as the training gym at school, so I went out and started to do some fight exercises with the wooden training dummies. I took care not to use my bad arm, but it was difficult not to push myself. All I could think of was Martin Bellock's dog shit face, and pounding it in with my claws.

I hadn't told Tresten the full truth about why I'd lost control on him. He'd insulted my family and threatened my brother—but when he'd degraded Vander's status as an omega like that, I'd taken it as a threat against Tresten as well. Honestly, it surprised me. The kneejerk reaction I'd had, the sudden protectiveness I'd felt towards Tresten, it was almost like it'd come out of nowhere.

But it hadn't, had it? I was already feeling—hounds of Hell, it felt weird to admit this—jealous. I didn't like seeing other alphas checking him out.

Why did I feel like this so suddenly?

Because we were married now? Because that meant, according to custom, he belonged to me?

Was that it? Or was it because I was starting to *actually* feel something for him?

I didn't want to believe that could be it. So then why couldn't I get him out of my head? Ever since what happened yesterday, he'd taken up hold in my mind. I saw those icy eyes of his, that piercing gaze that I used to think was snobby but now seemed so damn…

Fuck.

It seemed so damn *hot*.

. . .

I'd even dreamt about him last night.

Shifted to half-wolf, I let loose a flurry of strikes at the wooden dummy, ending with a finishing attack with my jaws. The wood was soft, and I ground my fangs into it a little harder than normal. I was pulsing with tension that just wouldn't go away.

What was he doing right now?

My mind suddenly went to all those horny alpha bastards in our class. I slammed my fist into the dummy, sending it flying across the arena.

Those fuckers better not be flirting with him.

I dropped down onto the dirt, my body slowly shifting back to human form. I groaned. "Dammit."

What if there was a chance... this could actually work out?

"Forget about it," I mumbled to myself. "He hates you, anyway."

If he *hated* me, then why did he agree when I'd said that our situation was turning out to not be so bad after all? Why did it seem like he was warming up to me?

I pounded my fist onto the dirt. Why the hell was this so fucking confusing? I'd never felt this way about any of the girls I'd been with before. I'd never felt so damn unsure of myself. If I liked them, I'd take them, and I could *always* tell how they felt about me. But with him... I had no idea. This was turning my brain inside out.

A part of me wanted to say fuck this recovery and go into class anyway. I could say that I wanted to stand around and watch the lessons, even if I couldn't participate. It wasn't unbelievable, only I was sure that there would be *someone* who would eventually notice me paying more attention to Tresten than the actual lessons. I really didn't like the idea of anyone going after Tresten—fighting, flirting, it didn't matter. I didn't want anyone to touch him.

Except... me?

The trees erupted with the screeches of startled birds when my fist made solid contact with the wooden dummy, splitting it down the middle with a loud crack.

No... there was no way I could show my face in class in my state. Not with my shoulder, and not with how I was feeling. The others would be able to smell the weakness on me. I wasn't going to chance that. I gathered up the two halves of the wooden dummy and carried them back to the house, feeling slightly pathetic.

I traded the trashed dummy for a new one from the supply room in the basement, and returned to the training yard for more exercises. I found myself unable to resist slipping out of my sling to try and give my gimped shoulder some light usage. What was the limit of my injury and my body's natural healing abilities? If I was going to be the best, I couldn't let an injury slow me down. In the heat of battle, you had to work with your wounds or else end up dead.

Three hours later, a spot of crimson started to bleed through the bandages, and my shoulder ached intensely. Maybe I'd pushed myself a little too hard. I slowly removed the bandages and checked my arm in the bathroom mirror. The wound had already mostly closed up, but it was red and nastily swollen. I cleaned the area with a towel before reapplying new bandages and stepping into the shower.

Steam quickly filled the room as the piping hot water streamed down my body. I had to take care not to get the bandages wet. Such a nuisance, but only I could be blamed for it. If I'd been quicker, with sharper reactions, this wouldn't have happened.

No... but something worse might've happened instead. What if I had landed my intended attack? What if I'd… killed him?

. . .

WED TO THE OMEGA

Shame flooded through me as I realized just how close I came to ruining *everything* for my family—and Tresten's.

What happened?

Control. I lacked control. I was too reactionary, relying too much on my gut emotions and intuition.

But why was Martin's shit talking able to get to me now, all of a sudden? It wasn't new. I'd been dealing with his shit for years. Everyone had. I was sure he'd made more heinous comments in the past.

So why now?

It's because of Tresten.

I slammed my palm against the shower wall in strained frustration. It was because of him. Something had changed inside me in the short time since our lives had been so suddenly thrown together. I could feel it. It was like... my wounded shoulder. Raw. Aching. Vulnerable.

And I didn't know what to do.

. . .

Closing my eyes, I turned my head up to the water. Its heat tingled my skin, caressing my muscles and the weight between my legs. A vision of Tresten flashed through my mind, and I actually welcomed it. I could no longer deny how thinking about him was making me feel. His ice blue stare was no longer annoying—it was fucking sexy as hell. Every hard edge of his body stood out in my mind's eye and made me thrum with desire. I felt the heat of my alpha wolf smoldering deep inside my soul, howling out for his fertile omega body. I realized that I wanted to take him. I wanted to feel him against me, feel his strong hands grasping me and the heat of his flesh on mine. I wanted to push myself into him and leave my seed inside of him, to fill him up with it and with my child.

My hand went to my cock, and squeezed around its fully hardened length. I quickly made myself come, groaning as the climax hit me. When I opened my eyes, his face continued to trail in my vision with the echoing fade of my orgasm. I shut the water off and stepped out of the shower. I toweled myself off, my cock still swollen and throbbing. I left the bathroom, ruffling my hair with the towel using my good arm, and strolled out to the kitchen to grab a glass of water. Orgasms always made me thirsty.

I obviously hadn't heard Tresten come home. Towel still draped over my head, I nearly dropped the glass I was holding when his shout echoed through the room. I spun around and saw him standing wide eyed, his bag still hung over his shoulder. His shocked gaze slid down from my face, to my chest to my…

. . .

"Shit." I quickly set the glass onto the counter and whipped the towel from my head to drape it over my exposed—and still throbbing—parts. "Tresten—"

He was already gone, and I heard the door of his room swing shut.

TRESTEN

"Slow down," I whispered to myself. "Slow down." I stood with my back against my bedroom door, my heart racing so fast that I thought I might collapse. With the way my legs were shaking, it certainly felt like I was about to keel over.

I tried to gather myself, but the image of Loch's naked body burned in my mind. His incredibly gorgeous, perfect, naked body.

And his erect cock.

A deep need pulsed through my body, like a current of electricity traveling down a wire. It spread out at my pelvis, just below my stomach, and arced out through the swelling heat between my legs. I bit my lip, clenching my knees together in an attempt to keep myself standing. I felt the pulse again, and tried not to gasp. My hand shot between my legs and I grabbed my hardening cock. It was almost painful. What the hell was this feeling? I'd *never* felt this before, this intense *want*. My head was starting to throb, not quite a headache but more like my heartbeat intensified in my skull, with every pulse crying out for *him*. To have him. To have him... inside of me.

I straightened myself up, taking deep and long breaths. *Calm down, Tresten. Just calm down.* Just seeing him exposed and *ready* like that had ignited something frighteningly primal inside me. Deep breaths. I was slowly getting myself under control, but I could still feel this aching need throbbing somewhere inside of me. This need to be filled, to be taken...

"Tresten," I heard him call out. "I'm sorry. I didn't know you were home."

Why had his cock been hard? What had he been doing when he was in the shower?

"I-I know," I called back, unable to keep my voice from shaking. "Put your damn clothes on."

Or don't. I don't care.

"Already did."

. . .

I took a deep breath and opened the door. After splashing some water on my face in the bathroom, I went back out to the kitchen. Loch was sitting on a stool at the center counter, a glass of water in front of him. His cheeks were flushed pink, and he looked up at me for a moment before returning his gaze to the glass. He wore a pair of sweatpants, but was still shirtless. I felt my heart start to beat a little faster again.

"Sorry," he muttered. "It's annoying to put a shirt on."

"It's fine," I said. "I can help you, if you want."

He shook his head. "Shoulder hurts."

I slowly came over to him, willing my heart to slow itself, but the spicy scent of his body wash wasn't helping. "Loch. It's bleeding."

He glanced down at his shoulder, the white bandage spotted with little points of red, and covered it with his hand.

"What did you do? You weren't using your arm today, were you?"

He looked embarrassed. "It's hard for me to just sit around and do nothing, knowing everyone is training in class."

. . .

"Dammit," I groaned. "It's just going to make it take longer to heal. And how am I going to train you if your arm isn't getting better?"

"You're right. I shouldn't have pushed it."

"You shouldn't be using it at all."

Suddenly, my mind was no longer on the moment of indecent exposure, and all nervousness vanished and was replaced with concern for him. *Idiot.* Didn't he realize how he was risking himself? I went back to my room and dug through my still unpacked moving boxes until I found what I was looking for—a small glass jar of reddish-orange liquid. Loch glanced at me questioningly when I came back into the kitchen, and I pulled out the stool next to him and sat down.

"Hey, what are you doing?" he asked when I started to undo his bandages. He leaned away from me. "I just changed those."

"And you did a crappy job. Let me help you. My dad studied healing and taught me some stuff. So, are you going to sit still, or do you want your shoulder to stay fucked up?"

He gave me a side glance and leaned back towards me. I'd never seen Loch so shy before. He must've really gotten embarrassed. I returned his gaze, and just to give him a hard time I gave him a sharp look of disapproval that slowly melted into a smile. He smiled back, and sat still while I unwrapped the bandages. He really had done a terrible job at re-applying them.

The wound was actually healing quickly, but had broken in one area and was red and swollen. I lightly ran my fingertips along the side of it. It was hot to the touch.

"This might sting a little bit," I said, unscrewing the jar of ointment. I dipped a finger into it and then applied it on the wound. Loch's cheek flinched.

"It feels tingly," he announced.

"This is a special healing ointment," I told him. "Dad made it for me before I started my training at FAS. I've never used it until now. Feel special."

"Thanks," he said.

"You need to bind the bandage tighter. The way you did it before was too loose."

"It's not the easiest thing to do when you only have one hand to do it with," he said.

. . .

"Next time, wait till I'm here and I'll help you." I went and got a fresh length of bandage and started to re-wrap his shoulder. "How does that feel? Too tight?"

He shook his head, and I could feel his eyes on my face. My heart started to thud heavily again, and I kept my gaze leveled on what I was doing. It was my turn to feel shy. I didn't want to meet his eyes. My thoughts were returning to what I'd seen earlier, and my body was responding. I felt that ache again, pulsing out like a light in darkness, slowly growing stronger and stronger… He was looking at me, and if I looked back, if I looked into his eyes, I didn't know what would happen. I could feel it pounding through my whole body—*if I looked back right at this moment, something between us* will *happen*.

"Tresten."

"Done," I said quickly, and moved away to wash my hands in the kitchen sink.

I could still feel Loch's penetrating alpha stare on the back of my head.

"Thank you," he said, after a beat of silence. That thick feeling that'd been in the air was clearing, and the ache was subsiding.

. . .

I turned around to face him. He was looking at my handiwork and running his fingers over the bandages. "It doesn't hurt as much," he said.

"The power of the ointment," I said, with a quick smile.

"I'll need to thank your dad. Or... maybe it's more appropriate to just call him 'Dad'? I guess he's my father now too."

"You don't have to. I mean, you can. If you want." I was taken by surprise. *Call him 'Dad'?* Where'd this come from? I felt my face go hot again. Strangely, I realized that I actually enjoyed the idea of Loch calling Dad, 'Dad.'

And I promised myself I would never admit it to him.

"You've already trained on your own today," I said, "and you've showered. So, I guess you're done for the day, then."

"Done? No. Hell, no. I've been waiting the entire day for you to come back so we can get started. I'm not done."

"With how you pushed your injury, I don't know if we should start today. It might—"

. . .

"No. We're training today. Please, Tresten." Loch had reached out and grabbed me by the wrist, but that wasn't what had caught me off guard—it was the look burning in his eyes. I stared back, wide eyed. I'd avoided his gaze earlier, now I was unable to look away. It made me feel weak, like my legs wouldn't be able to support my weight. I hated feeling out of control, but there was something pleasurable about it right now that I'd never experienced before…

"Alright," I said, finding my voice. I pulled my arm away from him. "We'll train. But promise me that you'll be mindful of your arm. I'm not going to be responsible if you fuck it up even more."

He grinned. "I promise."

"Out back, then."

We walked out to the training yard together, and I noticed how the dirt in the big circle had been disturbed in an explosive flurry. Where the wooden dummy stood, the ground was scattered with long splinters. Loch had obviously had a very busy day.

"What were you doing out here?" I asked,

He shrugged. "Basic shit. Wooden dummy training. Trying to speed shift. Working using my good arm."

. . .

"Well, stop. From here until you get better, no more of that. You're going to reinforce bad habits."

"What? I'll go insane if I don't do anything during the day. I mean, I'd rather train alone with you, but I can't just do *nothing*."

Alone with you. I felt that aching need pulse deep inside me again, and quickly did everything I could to push it away.

"Then practice what we do together. I know it's hard for you, but don't do anything dumb, okay, Loch?"

He put his palms up in mock surrender. "Your wish is my command."

I gave him a look, and then walked out into the center of the training circle, gesturing for Loch to stand opposite me. "Remember what I told you the other day about the key to speed shifting?"

"You said that it's about mind-state, and that I need to remove the mental blocks that keep me from accessing my wolf. Right?"

. . .

I nodded. "So? Have you figured it out yet?"

"Not a damn clue. I thought my mind was clear already."

"Everyone does have their limits. I'm not surprised yours is mental."

"Shut up."

"When you shift, you want your mind to be completely blank." I stripped down to my underwear, and Loch followed suit. "You ready? Three… two…"

I looked deep inside and found my wolf, and called on it to bound forward and take over my body. My mind was a blank chasm, a space completely open and ready for my wolf form.

I felt all my muscles reconfigure as the shift started, my bones rearranging and morphing into place. I felt my tail explode out from just above my behind, my ears pulling out into their canine form. And then…

An image of Loch, naked and fully aroused, exploded into my mind's eye. The real Loch was shifting in front of me, and the Loch in my head started to shift too. I saw his naked body changing, his human cock growing into a rigid, aggressive alpha wolf cock, dripping with precome and ready to take me, to impregnate me…

My heart started to hammer against my chest. My shift was nearly complete, just barely faster than Loch's. I felt my cock springing to life, and fought to control the fantasy that had clawed its way into my mind as my shift to full wolf form finished.

Loch's shift completed too, just a split second after mine. "Look at that," he said, his voice a throaty growl. "I got faster. I almost matched you." He sat down on his haunches to take weight off his injured front leg. His tongue lolled out and licked his chops, his lips pulling back to reveal his fangs in a canine grin. "Or… were you a lot slower?"

"I was slower," I admitted, my ear twitching in annoyance. "I've been handicapped lately." I didn't want to expand on it any further, and especially not clue Loch in to what had flashed through my mind to slow my shift down, but he spoke up.

"Because of your mark," he said, nodding towards the dark fur that streaked through the center of my head, between my ears. "Because you're in heat."

"Well," I stammered. "I… everything that's been happening. The arrangement. Lots on my mind." *Like your hard, alpha cock.*

. . .

"I know it's because you're in heat. What are you going to do about it? It's going to keep screwing with your performance, won't it? How are we going to get any training done?"

I was thankful that wolves couldn't blush. "I'm just going to have to deal with it," I said angrily. "It won't be going away anytime soon."

"That's too bad," he said. "I was hoping I'd actually get to learn something from you, but it looks like we're both gimped." He barked out a laugh.

A low, irritated growl emerged from my throat. "It doesn't matter how fast I shift, idiot. You still haven't learned that you need to control your mind. Don't you get that that's the reason why you're still as slow as you always were? Or why you were one snap of the jaws away from never fighting again? Don't you get how lucky you were that Martin only got your shoulder? You could've been *seriously* hurt..."

He straightened, and if there was any blasé left in his eyes I couldn't see it. "I know," he said.

"Then learn to control your mind. Don't let your emotions control your actions. What thought has been occupying your mind the most? You said you don't know what's blocking you, but I think you do. It's likely more obvious than you think."

Loch looked away.

"You don't need to say it out loud," I said. "Just take it, and then let it go. Now... do you think you can tag me?"

His red eyes flashed excitedly. "You're damn right I can."

"Then do it."

There was no hesitation. Loch leapt into a direct forward attack—and smashed his snout right into the dirt.

"Ouch," he groaned. He'd forgotten about his shoulder, and had landed his pounce evenly on both front paws. His injured leg had buckled immediately, unable to support him.

"See? That's what I'm talking about. Not thinking, only acting. How is it you haven't gotten this yet? Master Graffer has nagged you constantly about it."

He grunted and got to his feet. I didn't wait for him to indicate he was ready, and leapt into a forward attack, aiming right at his bad leg. He spun into defense, but again it was a move that was completely reactionary, relying on pivoting on his injured side. It crumpled and slammed onto the ground. I soared over him and gave him a little nip with my fangs.

"Tag," I said. "One point for me."

"Dammit."

He got up. I attacked. He dodged, and crumpled again. And again. Now I left myself wide open for him, but again I controlled his attack and bounded right over his back, landing behind him. I nipped his tail.

"At least you didn't face plant that time," I said.

He let out a frustrated bark, and went for the attack again. I dodged. *Come on, Loch. You have to realize that just attacking normally is not going to work with your leg the way it is.* "Remember the lesson that Master Graffer taught us about our weapons? An attack is only good if the opponent doesn't see it coming. I can see your attacks coming from a mile away. Mix it up."

Our back and forth went on for an hour. Loch managed to tag me once on the paw. I'd tagged him fifteen times. If he hadn't been injured, he would have been a challenge, even despite his tactical deficiencies—Loch had always been one to rely on brute strength, or on pure raw intuition to win, and usually it worked for him when all the cards were in his favor. I realized that having this injury could actually be a *benefit* for him. It could force him into changing how he fought—though with how stubborn he was, I was having my doubts that he *could* change.

The sun was going down. The orange light of dusk split through the trees, casting long shadows across the training circle. Both of us were exhausted and hungry, but neither one wanted to be the first to throw in the towel. As long as Loch would push, I would push too. He hadn't changed his tactics. He was testing different ways to launch his attack to try and find one that worked with his handicap, but really, they were all variations on the same strategy. How could he not realize what he was doing?

And to add to that, I could distinctly sense there was something holding him hostage. This wasn't the usual Loch, there was something new that was blocking him. "Come on," I urged, lunging into an attack. He dodged out of the way, sending his jaws up to try and catch my leg. I saw it coming a mile away and avoided him. "What is this? What's distracting you?"

He landed and spun around, taking care not to put weight on his bad leg. We both stood facing each other, our tongues hanging out the side of our mouths as we panted for breath.

"Nothing," he said. "Just shut up and keep going."

. . .

"Then why can't you hit me? This is way beyond your injury. If this were class, Master Graffer would've dismissed you a long time ago. So, what's going on, Loch?"

"I said, nothing."

"I don't get it. How are you this *weak?* You've never been this weak before. What kind of alpha are you? You're failing right now, you know that? You're *failing.*"

He let out a roar of frustration and charged at me. *Again? You'll have to do better than that.* Instead of dodging his attack, I bolted direct at him. I was tired, frustrated, and annoyed. I hadn't expected him to get *worse*. What the hell was wrong with him? Why was—

Loch didn't try to avoid my attack. He kept his path, shooting straight at me, lowering his head. I'd assumed he would dodge—it was too late for me to alter my attack.

Our bodies slammed together, the impact of our attacks shuddering through me and forcing the air from my lungs. The world became a whirl of dust and fractured sunlight as we hit the ground, rolling and tumbling across the dirt together until we came to a stop. Loch had managed to manipulate the fall to get me on my back, his paws pinning me down at the joints. His lips drew back, fangs bared. His bandages, which had stretched to accommodate his wolf form, had torn free. I saw blood dripping down his black fur.

"Loch, your shoulder…" I quickly started the shift back to human form.

He shifted too, and soon we were lying nearly naked, our skin matted with dirt. His hands were still gripping me by the shoulders, holding me down. Dark spots of blood spattered onto the dirt and onto my skin. "Your shoulder," I repeated. He seemed to not feel the re-opened wound. His red eyes bore down into mine, a streak of black hair falling across his dirt-smeared forehead. My chest heaved, not just because I was exhausted but because my heart had started to pound.

"It's you," he said. His voice was a low growl, so low that I barely heard him. "I don't know what the fuck is going on, but you've taken over my mind."

"W-what? Loch…" I tried to move, but he held me firmly to the ground. Even with his wounded shoulder he was shockingly strong.

"These past two days, I can't stop thinking about you. I can't stop myself from wanting you. How did this happen, Tresten? How did I go from barely being able to stand you to… to this? I just don't fucking get it. How did you gain this power over me?"

. . .

I stared up at him, my pulse racing. I felt bewildered, unable to find my voice. He gazed down at me, and I watched as his expression slowly softened. It seemed like the world had gone quiet, except for the soft whisper of the wind through the trees that surrounded the training yard.

Loch drew in a breath and spoke, his voice even and strong. "Just tell me, Tresten. Have you been feeling the same way? Am I alone in this?"

My heart was beating so fast I thought I might have a heart attack. I opened my mouth, but my voice was still nowhere to be found. I looked deep into his crimson eyes. I didn't need to speak. He saw all he needed there.

As Loch's lips met mine, stealing away my first kiss, I felt a powerful surge of energy course through my body. It shot through my muscles, tightening them as if I were in climax, and my back arched up off the ground like an invisible rope had pulled me up by the waist. The shock extended through my arms, and I flung them out and around Loch's neck, clinging to him. His tongue brushed against mine and flicked softly against my lips. The surge made its final stop—my mind. It felt like I blanked out, like everything had been removed except for one thing: *Loch*. Now that aching need exploded outward through me, grabbing hold of me as I grabbed hold of him. I pulled him to me, our lips crashing desperately together.

. . .

I want him.

How had this feeling taken hold of me so suddenly?

Taken hold of both of us?

Although I'd never kissed anyone before in my life, kissing Loch somehow felt like the most natural thing I could do, as natural as breathing. His hands drew from where they held my shoulders and slipped behind my neck and my waist, and the warm swell of his chest pressed against mine. I drew my fingers down his back, amazed at the way his skin felt. I was tangled up in a wash of bliss. How could this feel so good? Where had this come from?

We broke from our kiss, but our faces still hung close to each other. I could feel the tickle of his breath on my lips. I gazed deeply into his eyes. Those stubborn eyes of his had suddenly taken on a different look. They were gorgeous. They were filled with life. They were the eyes of an alpha wolf.

"I'll take that as a yes," he whispered.

"What is happening?" I wondered aloud, dazed.

"I don't know. I don't know, but it's been a very weird past couple of days for me."

. . .

I slowly drew my hands down Loch's back until they reached his waist, and then brought them around to the curves of his abs. I let them explore up to his pecs, my fingertips taking in the shape of him for the first time. My hands moved with curious hesitation—I could hardly believe what I was doing, but again, it felt so natural. My lips hung parted in wonder. "What is happening?" I repeated, my voice barely a hush.

Loch stood up, offering me a hand to help me to my feet. He quickly turned and went to grab our clothes. I suddenly realized that my cock was pushing hard against my underwear, tenting the tight fabric. I didn't try to hide it—in fact, I *wanted* Loch to see it.

I watched as he slipped into his pants, his back still turned to me. Then he came back over and offered me my clothes. His eyes stayed leveled at mine. "I think maybe it's time to go back inside," he said. "It's getting dark."

I nodded. "Yeah."

He turned and started to walk back to the house. I followed behind him, my mind spinning, the warmth of his lips still fresh on my own.

LOCH

The walk back to the house felt like fucking forever. My shoulder was throbbing madly, a streak of blood running down my arm. I walked ahead of Tresten, wondering if he'd come up to my side, but he never did. Our true feelings had been dragged out into the open. Really, it felt like they'd been dragged out from deep inside of us. At least, that's how I felt. My head was a mess. This whole thing had happened so damn fast, and now I wasn't sure what to do next.

I wanted him—that much I knew for sure.

Was it normal for feelings about someone to change quickly like this? I'd never had this happen to me before. I'd always been the type of alpha who knew who he wanted on first glance, and Tresten had never been on my radar. Hell, I don't think I'd *ever* had an omega on my radar before. But now, I wanted him. No, to say it like that put what I felt on the same level as all the females I'd been with in the past. This was different. *Completely* different. What I felt for Tresten now was so much stronger, so much deeper.

What was it exactly? It wasn't love, I knew that. It was something separate from love, separate, but somehow just as strong. This was something that I'd never experienced before. It was like… coming for the first time.

And what did Tresten feel about this whole thing? He was being so quiet. I glanced over my shoulder at him and saw that he was looking at me. Our eyes met, and I felt my heart jolt. I quickly looked ahead again.

I wanted to kiss him again. I wanted to feel his touch again, his fingers on my skin. But… for some reason, even though we'd just kissed, I was having a hell of a hard time convincing myself to reach out to him again.

This is so… weird.

We made it to the back door, and I opened it to let him go in first.

"Thank you," Tresten said. He stopped, his eyes widening. "Your arm." He reached out, but didn't touch the wound. "I'm sorry. That was my fault. And here I was telling you not to strain it."

. . .

"It's fine," I said. "I'll just use a bit more of that magic ointment."

He gave me a thin smile, and I could see in his eyes that he was as mixed up about this as I was. When he passed by me and walked inside, I caught the scent of his hair and I felt my legs go a little weak.

"Let me clean it for you," he said. "Sit down." He nodded towards the kitchen counter, and I went and took a seat on one of the stools. Tresten went to his room and came back out with a full first aid kit, and set it onto the counter.

"Definitely going to need to take better care while training," he said. "I shouldn't have pushed you like that."

I couldn't stop myself from inhaling a sharp breath of surprise when he stepped in close to me, sliding between my thighs. My body stiffened, unsure what to do. He started to clean my wound, his focus locked on what he was doing. His face was so close to mine, a sweep of white hair hanging down over his forehead. He started to clean the wound, and I ignored the pain. My attention was on him, and those beautiful eyes of his.

"Are you sure you're not fucking me up on purpose, so that you can keep doing this for me?" I teased. His blue eyes shot up and he gave me a playful scowl and nudged a finger into my shoulder. "Ahh! Ouch."

"Quiet."

I obeyed, sitting silently while he did his work. *This is totally unnecessary,* I realized. *I could've cleaned it myself in the shower.* My body relaxed, and my hands regained control. Slowly, my fingers found his thigh. I felt the slightest shiver when I made contact, but that was the only recognition that I'd touched him. He kept working on my wound.

I let my fingers make their way upwards, moving along the back of his thigh until I reached the curve of his ass. He blinked, but kept working, still otherwise ignoring my exploration. It wasn't until I slipped my hand underneath his shirt and pulled him in closer to me that he stopped what he was doing. The front of his thighs pushed against my crotch, and my face was up against the flat of his stomach. I craned my neck to look up at him. He grabbed my shoulders to steady himself, and looked down at me. Then, with my hand still caressing the small of his back, I guided him down until he was sitting on my thigh, his arms wrapped around my neck.

He leaned down and kissed me. I hungrily tasted his lips and tongue again, a rush of excitement swelling my cock so that it pushed painfully against the inside of my underwear. Tresten dropped the swab he was holding and caressed my cheek.

. . .

"*Something* is happening," I said with a little grin when our lips separated.

"Tell me about it." He stood up, picked the swab off the floor, and then packed up his first aid kit. "I… should shower. You should too. We're covered in dirt, and it's late."

"Sure," I said.

Tresten picked up the kit, and his hand lingered on my arm as he moved to leave. I watched him, my cock still throbbing and hard. *I'm going to have to empty the pipes in the shower or else I'll go insane*, I thought. He made his way over to his side of the house, his tight little ass sashaying slightly as he walked. *How had I never noticed how fucking sexy he was before?*

He stopped in the doorway, took a single glance back at me, and then slipped out of the room.

Fuck. I exhaled a long breath that I felt like I'd been holding for an hour.

Everything felt different now. Even this house seemed to have changed. Only a few hours ago, I would've said the place felt like a prison, and the idea that Tresten and I would be spending the rest of our lives together? Insanity. Now, after that kiss…

. . .

It was like a spell had descended over me, and over everything.

Well, Loch. The impossible has happened. You've fallen for someone. I don't know how it's possible, I don't know how things could've changed fucking fast, but there it is. There's no denying it.

Was this… fate?

I'd grown up with bedtime stories of fated mates and all that, everyone had, but I don't think I ever believed that there was any truth to those tales. It sure as hell felt real now, though. How else could I explain the sudden shift in our relationship? My heart continued to pound solidly in my chest, and my lips tingled from our second kiss. They were thirsting for a third, and my cock, still hard with want, was thirsting for something else.

I heard the shower turn on in Tresten's bathroom, and I imagined him stripping off his clothes, letting the water wash the dirt from his bare skin. Then I saw that look that he gave me as he left, his icy eyes flashing like blue crystals backlit by fire. Was it a look of invitation?

I rose to my feet. My legs carried me forward towards his room, and towards the sound of the running shower. It almost felt like my body was moving on its own, taking me to him. I unfastened the button of my pants as I walked, dropped them to my ankles, and stepped out of them. I entered his room for the first time. His unpacked moving boxes still cluttered the floor, almost as if he expected he wasn't going to be staying for long. The bathroom door was ajar, a wisp of steam hazing out from the top. I could hear the drum of water against the shower floor, and I caught a glimpse of Tresten's silhouette reflected in the bathroom mirror. My cock pulsed, and I removed my underwear.

I was completely naked. I strode confidently to the door and pushed it open. Tresten's body was a rippled haze through the water streaked glass of the shower door. Without speaking a word, I opened it and stepped inside behind him.

The water poured down over me, and I drew my arms slowly around Tresten's waist. His hands leapt to mine and grabbed them. I thought he was going to yank them away, to maybe turn and strike me in the face, but he only held them there. "What are you doing?" he said.

"Showering, what does it seem like I'm doing?"

I pulled him against me, and my hard cock slid up against his wet skin, following the crease of his ass. My pecs pressed against his back, and I buried my face into his neck and kissed him there, the water pouring down over my head.

"Who said you could come to my side of the house? Use your own fucking shower," he murmured. I felt his body start to tremble slightly, despite the heat of the water. His hand moved from mine, and I gasped when it slipped between us and wrapped firmly around my length. I groaned in pleasure when he started to move his hand. My teeth raked against his neck, and I slowly reached down until my hand found his member. He was standing rock hard. I gripped him. It was the first time I'd ever held another man's cock, and for a moment I couldn't help but notice how familiar, yet different it was from my own. I explored it fully, getting to know its girth and length and shape.

This is really happening. Tresten and I are doing this together.

His free hand reached back and pulled my head closer to him as he tilted his head back and kissed me. Our tongues probed and explored, and our hands continued their work. Tresten moaned onto my lips and started to buck his hips as I stroked him. "I'm going to come," he cried. "Oh, shit…"

His body tensed and his fingers clenched at my hair. I felt his cock pulse and stiffen in my grip, and I watched as he shot his load against the shower wall. He slackened. Then he turned around and dropped to his knees, his hand still wrapped around my dick. I looked down at him, and he returned my gaze with his icy blue eyes. I licked my lips. Tresten licked his. Then he opened wide and took me into his mouth.

My eyes rolled back and I let out a long groan. "Fuck…"

. . .

It was obvious that Tresten had never done this before, but it didn't matter. Just the fact that it was *him* doing it was enough. I could never have imagined this scenario in my wildest dreams—let alone *loving it*. I looked down and watched him do his best to pleasure me with his mouth, and it was the moment that he looked up at me with those eyes of his that I felt the orgasm coming.

I tossed my head back and growled out a strained moan as I came, fireworks exploding across my vision. The sound of the shower drowned out and was replaced by a pitched whine. My cock throbbed, and Tresten took it all. I helped him to his feet, and pulled him tightly against me. We kissed, the water cascading down over our heads.

"I've never done that before," Tresten breathed.

"This has been a day of firsts for the both of us, Tresten," I said. The haze of the orgasm was fading, replaced by that feeling of bewilderment. "I think we have a thing or two to talk about."

"Yeah. I'd say we do."

After we finished showering, Tresten re-applied ointment to my wound and re-dressed it, then cooked dinner—more steak. We ate in silence for a while, both of us unsure of what to say.

. . .

I spoke first. "I thought you hated me."

He looked up from his plate. "Maybe I still do."

I gave him a look. "Come on."

"I didn't think you were such a big fan of me either."

"I wasn't. I mean, I didn't hate you. But you know how I felt about you."

"You thought I was a brat."

"That's about right."

He sighed. "I'm not used to this. This all feels so weird to me. I don't regret what we did one bit, but it felt like everything just came out of nowhere. The change happened in me so quickly."

"Hey, I'm no more used to this than you are."

Tresten eyed me. "Yeah, but you've been with plenty of people before, so you at least know what it feels like…"

. . .

"Not even comparable," I said firmly. "Not one bit. I've… Dammit, I've never felt like this before about anyone."

"Me neither," he said. "Honestly, I was a little worried that this was just business as usual for you."

"Believe me, it's not. It started before, but yesterday after the fight, when I had to come back early, I couldn't stop thinking about you. When Martin said those things about my brother, it felt like he was saying it about all omegas. It felt like he was saying it about *you*. The thought of Martin doing anything to you… I wanted to protect you."

"I don't need you to protect me, Loch," Tresten said. "I can take care of myself." He thought for a moment, then smiled. "But I do appreciate it."

"I know you don't," I said. "I know you could kick anyone's ass in our class. But I still couldn't help but feel that way. Protective. I guess, it's because you're my husband now. I don't know. I'd convinced myself that I would do everything I could not to let this arrangement change my life, in whatever way that I could help it. But now without even expecting it, it's changed everything. Suddenly, I'm… Fuck." I froze up, the words caught in my mouth. Tresten waited patiently.

"Suddenly, I'm crazy about you, Tresten. Explain to me how something like this fucking happens in a day."

. . .

His face went pink, and he ran his fingers through his white hair. Adorable.

"I want to know the same thing. I don't think there is an explanation. It just happened. When you told me about your family, and about your feelings as a third alpha, and how you fought against Martin to defend those feelings, that was what really changed things for me. So, I guess I'm the same. Perhaps we ought to be thanking Martin Bellock for what he did. Maybe this wouldn't have happened if it weren't for him."

I scowled. "I will never thank that piece of dog shit."

Tresten bit his lip and grinned at me.

"No, I think it's obvious this would've happened even without Martin. Maybe it would've taken longer, but I was already feeling things about you before that."

He nodded. "Yes, you're right. So… I suppose our parents will be happy to hear that things are working out."

I laughed. Mom and Dad. They definitely would be relieved to know that Tresten and I weren't at each other's throats. To hear that we were actually *falling* for each other? It was hard for me to imagine their reaction.

. . .

No, that's not true. I knew exactly what their reaction would be. They'd press me about the second part of the contract, and I was sure that Tresten's parents—*Dad and Pa, I mean*—would feel the same way.

They'd want to know about our plans to start a family. To have a kid.

"We probably should arrange a family meeting," I said.

"And... what's next for us?"

I paused, wondering if Tresten was thinking about the same thing as I was. The idea felt so foreign to me. I'd imagined myself having a kid at some point in my life, but I figured it would've been *after* I became a master. At the very least, after graduating from the FAS. It was difficult to think about having one with Tresten, despite how things had changed between us. I was only just getting to understand who he was.

And knowing what I knew about him, how would *he* feel about the idea? Having a child would mean having to leave the school. It'd mean having to *abandon the fighting arts*.

Could I see him doing that?

. . .

Hell, no. Tresten was the most dedicated fighter in our class, and he was fucking determined to make it as an omega fighter. I could never imagine him abandoning his training for a child.

Even if this arrangement depended on it?

No child, no heir to protect his family's position. No heir, and our arrangement would be meaningless for the Crocs. Even I understood that. And if the arrangement became meaningless for them… what would that mean for my family? Would the Crocs and Lunas divide again?

Would Tresten and I be separated?

I didn't know. Maybe I was getting ahead of myself.

I smiled, trying to cover up my thoughts. "We… take things slow."

TRESTEN

When shifted into the half-wolf form, a fighter's senses and physical strength are increased by a hundred-fold. Hyper sensitive hearing gives the ability to detect the way an attack is moving, from which direction and how fast, allowing the fighter to do things impossible for a normal human. With increased muscular density and animal ferocity, a punch or a claw attack from a half-wolf shift can be delivered with devastating force. The ability to defend against these attacks through utilizing increased senses all depends on the user's mind. Are your thoughts clear? Focused? Distraction free?

My head snapped to the side as the fist connected with my snout, knocking an explosion of galaxies into my vision. *Ouch.*

Obviously, I was not clear, focused, or distraction free.

. . .

My whole body followed my face, spinning around in one corkscrew turn before slamming onto the dirt of the FAS training ground.

"What the fuck is going on with you, Croc?" Master Graffer shouted. "Get up!"

I tried to shake away the spinning lights, my head throbbing as I got to my feet. My opponent had gotten me good. The world would not stop whirling, and I fell back flat on my ass.

"Alright, alright, enough. That's a match." Master Graffer walked over and yanked me to my feet. He eyed me up and down. "Go take a break. You're bleeding, go bandage your face and get a drink of a water."

I shifted back to human form and touched my cheek. It throbbed painfully, and my fingers came away red. *Damn.* I really wasn't myself. But who could blame me? My thoughts were far, far away from fighting, for the first time ever. As I slunk out of the room, I felt the eyes of the class watching me. They'd no doubt talk shit—I'd already overheard some whispers and murmurs about how me being in heat was proof that an omega didn't belong in the FAS. It pissed me off, but at the same time… I was beginning to wonder if it was true. The decline in my abilities had been so obvious, and now with what was happening between Loch and me?

. . .

Maybe that was why there were so few omega masters. How could I deny my own biology?

In the locker room, I dug out the first aid box and cleaned up the small gash on my cheek in front of the mirror. My thoughts went immediately to Loch. I saw him there in the reflection, imagined him standing next to me, putting his hands on me, his lips searching my neck while his fingers went down…

A shiver of excitement rose all the hairs on my body.

This morning, I'd found Loch in the kitchen doing his best to cook with one free arm. He made me his own special pre-training breakfast, and sent me off to class with a kiss. *A kiss.* I could hardly believe how happy it all made me. Had I ever felt that kind of happiness before? I doubted it. This had taken me completely by surprise. It almost didn't feel real.

And look how that happiness was affecting me. Bashed in the face. Shift getting even slower. But every time I tried to concentrate, I just saw him there. I just wanted to feel his touch again. I wanted to go home and see him. I wanted to explore his body, and him to explore me. It'd all felt *so good*. It was like the thrill of the most intense fight—no, it was better. *The rush!* I wanted Loch to show me all the things I'd been missing out on, avoiding relationships for training. I wanted him to make me his, completely and entirely.

. . .

What would it feel like?

I'd always been the type of wolf who had to be in control of things. I wasn't like those typical delicate omegas. I'd never liked the idea of having an alpha tell me what to do. *I* was the boss. So what would it be like to have Loch… dominate me?

What would it be like to have him bend me over and take me? To spread my ass cheeks wide and do things to me that I never could've imagined myself enjoying?

I wanted him to do everything to me.

The locker room was quiet, except of the gentle hum of the overhead lights. I closed my eyes and let the fantasy take over my mind.

What would he do to me…? I'd always thought that him shifting out his ears and tail to try and look cute was the stupidest thing, but now I wanted to see him do it. He would look so sexy like that. I wanted to do it too. I wanted him to come up behind me, grab my tail and…

The sound of the locker room door opening pulled me out of my thoughts. I spun around and saw two janitors make their way inside. One was in wolf form and had bags of cleaning supplies strapped over his back, the other was pushing a rolling bucket of water with a mop in it. They both looked surprised to have found someone inside the locker room.

"Er, hi. Sorry, I'll leave," I said, and shuffled out. I glanced at the clock—I'd been standing in front of that mirror for twenty minutes.

I made my way down the hallway back to the training arena, big splashes of afternoon sunlight falling across the stone floor. I sighed a dreamy sigh, and just about kicked myself. I needed to get ahold of myself, but it felt like my attention was… well, it was locked by Loch. Every moment, it seemed like his stupid handsome face was pushing its way into my focus. I rubbed my swollen cheek. A reminder of what happened when attention was diverted.

"Tresten?"

I froze. Hounds of Hell. Had Loch taken over my mind to the point where I was *hearing* his voice in my head now?

"Tresten."

Footsteps from behind me. I turned around and an embarrassing little squeak of surprise escaped from my mouth. Loch strode towards me, a big grin on his face, a canvas bag draped over his good shoulder. "Hey," he said.

"What are you doing out of class?" His eyes narrowed in concern. "What the hell happened to your cheek?"

"Loch? What are you doing here?"

"I was going insane sitting at home. So, I cooked you lunch—us lunch." He held up the bag. "A picnic, out on the lawn. Call it… a date?" He gave me a sheepish smile, the cheeky one that I remembered him giving girls in the hallway before. It was a smile that I'd thought was irritating and the opposite end of attractive, but right now, it was the most adorable thing I'd ever seen.

I started to protest. "You should be resting—" He cut me off with a hug. A big, one armed, very public, hug. "You're hugging me."

"I'd be doing a whole lot more if we were back home," he said, and I felt warmth pulse between my legs. I pushed away from him.

"Loch, we're in school. People could see." I looked around. The hall was still empty.

"Is that a problem?"

"Well, no… I just… I didn't think you'd want people to see."

. . .

"It's true, I didn't before. But people are going to know about us eventually, right?"

"Yeah."

He gave me a look. "So, what's the problem, then?"

"I don't know." Everything was happening so quickly, I hadn't even thought about bringing what was happening between us into the public yet. I already would have to deal with my decline in abilities, and to have the entire class know that Loch and I were married—and intimate? "I guess I'm not sure if I'm ready."

Loch looked surprised and hurt. He took a half step back from me and the bag slid down his wrist. "I'm getting carried away," he said. It sounded like he was admonishing himself. "Swept up in whatever this craziness is that's happened between us. Yeah, I guess I am."

His change in expression, from that smile to the cloudy look he wore now, socked me right in the heart.

"You're right, Tresten. I shouldn't have… We said we'd take it slow. Things would become complicated if people found out, especially for you. I wasn't thinking." He handed the bag to me. "Well, I did make you lunch. Chicken pesto sandwiches. I went grocery shopping today."

. . .

"Thank you," I said. "That's really nice of you." I was holding it down, but really, I wanted to just give him a big kiss. He made a picnic for us. *Why am I being so reserved all of a sudden?*

"Who did that to your cheek?" he asked.

"Kyle Lanley. I let my guard down."

Loch chewed his teeth. "Bastard."

I gave him a look. "Everyone gets injured sometimes. Loch. I told you, I don't need protecting. It's not flattering."

He blinked, and then relaxed. "Right. I can't really help it. I guess it's a kneejerk reaction. I really don't like the idea of anyone touching you, in any way."

I smiled. "Well, thanks. I guess I can appreciate the sentiment."

The easygoing, roguish smile returned to his face. "Well, guess I'll see you back at home then. Train hard." He looked like he was about to hug me again, but instead he thrust his hands into his pockets before turning to walk away.

. . .

The bag of lunch in my hand, I watched my husband leave. The pools of sunlight washed over him like the eye of some heavenly creature. I realized I didn't want him to go. I realized I didn't care what people thought.

"Loch!" I called. He stopped and looked back at me. "Wait for me outside. I'll come out for you after the lesson is over."

His easygoing smile widened into a grin brighter than the clearest sunlight.

* * *

I found him laying on a bench in the shade of a huge, ancient oak tree right outside the FAS building. He had his arm covering his eyes, and from his breathing I could see that he was asleep. I knelt down next to him and, without hesitating, left a kiss on his lips. He smiled and stirred, moving his arm so that he could see me.

"Well, I definitely could get used to waking up like that."

"Sorry to keep you waiting," I said.

He sat up and stretched. "You have no idea how fucking weird it feels to not be inside training with everyone else. It's torture. Almost as bad as waiting to see you."

. . .

I felt my face go hot. Loch seemed to have such an easy time saying things like that. It seemed so natural to him. I, on the other hand, was still trying to get used to *us*. Three days into my feelings for him, and only a day since everything changed, I felt like my reaction had to be the more grounded one. He'd transitioned so easily.

We walked together across the campus towards the grassy square. I walked on Loch's right side—his good side—and he carried the bag of food in his right hand. I couldn't deny how good it felt to walk side by side with him, to feel him next to me and know he was with me. I snuck a glance at his hand. "Let me carry that," I said, and took the bag from him and slung it over my other shoulder. Then, as my heart pattered nervously in my chest, I reached over and took his hand. He looked at me and then squeezed my palm.

Looking around, I saw plenty of other couples strolling around campus hand in hand, and it made me warm inside to realize that Loch and I were now one of them. I really had never expected to enjoy this feeling before, a feeling that I'd never even knew existed until now. It was like I was walking on air.

We made it to the grassy square. It was busy today, with lots of other couples lounging around and eating lunch. Not a surprise, considering how beautiful a day it was. We found our own patch of grass and sat down, and I slipped the bag from my shoulder and opened the plastic container inside. In it were two sandwiches, perfectly sliced into triangle halves. I was greeted by the rich smell of green pesto and chicken, and my stomach immediately started to rumble.

"It's probably not the best food to eat for training," Loch said.

I took a bite and just about died at the explosion of deliciousness. "Maybe not," I said with my mouth full, "but it tastes amazing."

Loch looked happy. We sat quietly, enjoying the food and each other's company. Even though the square was filled with students enjoying time between classes, I was hardly paying attention to them. Neither of us were. We had begun to slip away into a world where only the two of us existed.

"Hey, Loch," I said, after we finished eating.

"Yeah?"

"Can we try something?" I asked, feeling slightly embarrassed.

"Try what?"

. . .

I'd always seen couples out here lounging around together, with one of them shifted into wolf form while the other lay nuzzled into their side, still in human form, like they had a gigantic wolf pillow. I used to see it and think it was cheesy, but now I wanted to try it. I told Loch, and he laughed.

"I didn't think you'd be into something so stereotypical."

"Stereotypical!" I punched his good shoulder. "Give me a break. I've never been with anyone before, remember?"

He stroked my hair, and then pulled me against him in a hug. My face buried into his chest, I was washed in his warm scent, completely surrounded by him. "You'll have to give me a hand with getting my shirt and pants off," he said. "I don't want to ruin these clothes."

I helped him remove his clothes down to his underwear, and then folded them neatly for him. Loch sat down onto the grass, looking like he was ready for a day at the beach, and then shifted. He took his time with the shift, not worrying about speed-shifting like during our training. I watched as he brought out his wolf ears and tail first, and then his face, and the rest of his body, until he was in fully shifted. Loch's wolf form was huge, as most alpha male wolves were. I could probably ride on his back in my human form, and even in my wolf form, I was smaller than him. He leaned his weight onto his right paw, and then stretched out onto the soft grass. He lowered his head down, and I stroked the area between his ears, loving the feeling of his fur between my fingers.

. . .

"Go on," he said. "Don't be shy about it."

I lay down and rested my head against his side. He was so warm, and I rose and fell with each of his breaths. I stared up at the clear sky above us, and a pleasant wind shuffled the grass and ruffled Loch's fur and my hair. I was thinking about what was happening between us, the impossibility of it all.

After some time, I thought that maybe Loch had fallen asleep, so I said his name softly.

"Tresten," he said. His voice rumbled through his entire body and into my ears.

"I don't get it. How are you so adjusted? It seems like this is all so normal for you."

"No, it's anything but normal."

"I feel so hesitant. Maybe it's because I've never been with anyone before."

"And I've never felt this way about anyone before," he said, making my heart skip a beat.

. . .

"Then how are you making this seem so normal for you?"

"Does it bother you?" he asked.

I knew Loch was experienced with relationships and had been with plenty of girls before, so I only assumed that that was the reason why he seemed to be taking this so easily. Loch's playboy nature had always irritated me before, but that was before I'd gotten to know him, before I'd actually spent time with him. So, did it bother me?

"I guess, I just wonder if this is just all business as usual for you. If this is how it is with all of the people you've been with."

"You don't like that I've slept around," he said. "I always had a feeling that was part of the reason why you were always so cold to me."

I felt embarrassed—embarrassed for judging him and for never giving him, or anyone else, a chance. "Yes, it was," I admitted.

"Totally understandable."

. . .

He took a big breath, and I rose and fell like a boat on a wave.

"I know that my parents care about me, but they've never been the type to show much affection. Or, maybe they do it in their own way. They were always tough on all of us, but especially me. I never blamed them. I'm the third alpha. My role in my family was always a big question mark. When we started having our financial problems, things became worse, and I felt like a burden being at home. So, turning to girls was a way to get myself away from family. It wasn't the best thing for me to do, but I did it."

"So it was all a distraction," I said.

"Distraction, an escape… a way out."

I poked him in the ribs. "Couldn't you have done something more productive? You could've trained harder, and maybe you wouldn't be such a slow shift."

He snorted. "Yeah, but training isn't nearly as fun."

"I see."

He curled his head around to look at me. "You probably think I'm a shitty person, huh?"

. . .

"Just a little," I teased, and he chuckled.

"You're different, Tresten," he said, his voice serious now. "I hope you can believe me—and trust me."

I nodded. "I do. You have honor, Loch. I've learned that about you. I trust you. And I trust us. I'm not going to doubt what's happening with us anymore. I'm not going to question it. I'll trust it."

His eyes softened, and he nuzzled his huge snout against me. I laughed, and hugged my arm around it. We lay there together for the rest of the break. When it was time to go back, Loch shifted back to human form, and the two of us made our way back to the FAS building holding hands. When we neared it, Loch looked at me questioningly, and I felt his grip loosen on mine. I returned his look with one of confidence—*I know what I want now. I'm not afraid of it.*

We walked into the main hall together, hands still clasped, in full view of the entire class.

LOCH

*W*alking into that hall with Tresten was one of the most exciting things I'd ever done. I felt all eyes turning to us. I saw the shocked faces of my friends and the guys I trained with, the same guys who refused to give Tresten the respect he deserved just because he was an omega. They were all guys who respected me, and I wanted them to see and know how I felt about the man next to me.

From all the murmuring and whispering, one dog shit voice, the voice that I'd been waiting for, called out.

"Look at this!" Martin strolled out to block our way, his snickering cronies behind him. "Fuck, Luna. Did I fuck you up that bad?" He tapped his head. "I never thought you would be an omega lover."

"Fuck off, Bellock," I grunted. "Go chew a bone."

. . .

We tried to pass him, but he moved to stop us. A small crowd had started to form, the smell of a fight on the air.

"Maybe I shouldn't be surprised," he said. "Every fucker in the class was hounding after that tight omega ass. Hell, even I wouldn't mind taking a taste."

Everything seemed to go numb throughout my whole body. Then hot, like lava was smoldering in my skull. I saw red. *I'm going to kill him. I'm going to fucking kill him.* I didn't care that my left arm was still fucked. I wasn't even thinking about it. I took a step forward—and then felt Tresten's hand on my chest. He pushed me back. Immediately, my mind cleared. I looked at him, and was startled by the ferocious intensity in his ice blue eyes. They bore down brutally on Martin like frozen daggers. It was the kind of penetrating stare that could stop an opponent in their tracks, and I saw Martin actually take a full step back. His expression changed, and he immediately tried to cover up his shock.

I'd never seen Tresten, or *anyone* in our class give a look like that before. There was no anger. It was just all calm, neatly packaged and highly focused killing intent. I'd only ever seen that look from the eyes of master fighters.

"Watch your mouth," Tresten said. His voice projected out, filling the hall. "Let me remind you where you stand, *Bellock*. The Blood Gulch Clan might have bought their way into power, but you're still nothing next to the elder clans. The Ice River Pack and The Crescent Moon Pack are united because of Loch and my marriage. Even someone as vacant headed as you can understand what that means."

I could see by the snarl on Martin's face that he did. With our combined strength, the alliance between our families made our clans two of the most powerful in the country. Martin's parents would now need to touch their noses to the ground in respect to our clans, or else risk being shunned and ruined.

"Now, we can forgive you for what you've said about me," Tresten continued. "But what you did to Loch's shoulder was unacceptable. There's a score to be settled." He glanced at me, and I realized where he was going with this.

"What score," Martin said, his voice a low growl. Earlier, he'd been trying to draw a crowd. Now it seemed like he didn't want anyone to hear us. Tresten had completely gutted him without having to lift a finger. "What do you want?"

"Payback," I said. "I challenge you to an official fight, with our clan leaders as witness."

Martin straightened up, and that look of dumb arrogance appeared again. Then he started to laugh. "Seriously? How are you going to fight, you're all fucked up. Oh, I get it. You want me to lose on purpose, to get your dignity bag in front of mommy and daddy, is that it?"

"No. A fair, clean fight," I said. "After my arm heals."

"And when I beat your ass to the ground? Then what happens? I get to fuck him?" He nodded to Tresten, and I did everything I could to control the rage. Tresten touched my arm.

"No," said Tresten. "Better. If you win, I'll resign from the FAS."

My mouth dropped open. "Wait, what?"

Martin broke into another fit of ugly laughter. "Shit. No more weak-ass omega taking up space in my school? Deal."

I tried to protest, but Tresten held up his hand. "And if you lose, you will leave the FAS."

He snorted. "Fine. So, when am I going to be destroying you, Loch?"

"Tresten?" I asked. "Since it's your future on the line."

. . .

"Two months," he said. "Two months to heal and to train." He directed his final comment to Martin. "And you'd better train hard. Because Loch *is* going to kick your ass."

* * *

That night, Tresten invited his best friend over to meet me, and to fill her in on all the crazy shit that'd happened with us over the past couple days. Velvy was a slightly bookish girl with shoulder length brown hair, yellow eyes, and an infectious smile. The moment she walked in the front door, she eyed me up and down, socked me on the chest, and told me I was hot. "No wonder you were able to get through Tresten's impenetrable armor."

"Hey, get your eyes off my husband," Tresten laughed.

We sat in the living room, Tresten leaning against me with my arm around him as we told her about the challenge we'd made to Martin Bellock.

She gaped. "You cannot be serious. Tresten, why would you make a deal like that? Risking everything for some honor? I don't get you fighters. Nothing you guys do makes sense. Especially the fighting."

"Loch won't lose," Tresten said. "I'm going to make sure of it. I'm training him."

. . .

"But Tresten," Velvy said. "You're not a master. You're really going to put your training on the line for Loch?" She turned to me. "No offense."

I shook my head.

"He won't lose," he repeated. "Loch is already good enough to beat Martin. His technique is better, he has better intuition."

"Thanks, Tresten," I said. "I think that's the first time I've heard you really compliment my skills."

He smiled at me. "There are certain things holding him back, and I think I can help him get through them."

Velvy looked skeptical, and I didn't blame her. "Do *you* think you'll be able to beat that guy?" she asked me.

"I'll have to," I said. "I have no choice. I'm not going to be responsible for Tresten quitting school."

She shook her head. "I really don't get fighters."

Later, when Tresten had left the room to use the bathroom, Velvy spoke to me quietly. "I could never have imagined him doing something like this," she said. "He did it for you, you know? So that you'd train your hardest."

"Yeah," I said. "I realize that. I'm not happy about it, I tried to convince him to change his mind and alter the terms."

"He is really stubborn. But he obviously cares a lot about you. I don't know what's more surprising to me—Tresten actually falling in love with someone, or him putting his training on the line."

Love? Was Tresten in love with me?

I felt warm tingles of excitement spread through my entire body. Was it too early for me to admit that I was in love with him? I felt so strongly about him already, but after him confronting Martin… seeing how incredible he was, how strong, how *perfect*—it'd become immediately obvious to me that Tresten was my soulmate. It was the only explanation for everything that was happening, and how damn perfect he was for me.

I was in love with him. Painfully in love.

After Velvy left, Tresten and I both called our parents to inform them that we needed to have an official family meeting to bring them up to speed with everything. We agreed to have a joint meeting during the weekend at the Croc family house.

"I'm worried about what your parents will think about this challenge. I feel responsible."

"They'll understand," Tresten said. "I know Pa would've done the exact same thing for Dad if they were in the same situation."

I took his hands in mine. "I'm not going to lose," I said. "I'll win, for us."

He gave me a determined grin. "And I'll put *everything* into making sure you do."

We kissed, and I felt that flame deep down inside me burning hot for him. It grew and grew, and my hands tugged at his shirt, pulling him in tight against me. Tresten sighed softly against my lips. He slipped his hands around my waist and pressed his hips against mine. I could feel his excitement against my thigh. I could tell that this had been on his mind the entire day. It'd been on my mind too. Sitting at home while he was in class, I'd couldn't go even one second without thinking about having his lips on mine again. I tried to recall every detail of our moment in the shower, and of how his wet, naked body felt against mine. I wanted to explore him and be explored by him. I wanted to take him and make him mine, to feel him all around me.

. . .

He moaned when I brought my lips to the soft flesh of his earlobe, and then down to the curve of his neck. He smelled amazing.

"Loch," he murmured. "Can you do something for me?" There was an adorable shyness in his tone.

"Tell me."

"You know… that thing you'd do sometimes at school? I'd see you shift so that you'd have just your wolf ears and your tail out. Could you do that?"

"Oh, you like that, huh?"

"Uh-uh. I thought it was intolerable."

I laughed. My wolf ears emerged first, pushing up from out of my hair. Then I pulled down the back of my pants to let my tail come free.

"You look so silly," Tresten said before kissing me again. "Little puppy boy." He stroked my ears, and I closed my eyes to enjoy the bliss of it.

. . .

With my wolf ears, I could easily hear the steady thud of Tresten's excited heartbeat, calling me to him. "Come here," I said, and grabbed him around his thighs beneath his ass with my good arm and muscled him up over my shoulder.

"Ah! Loch!"

I strode over to the living room couch and tossed him onto it. I pounced after him, and Tresten threw his arms and legs around my body. He tore at my clothes, yanking them from my body. I did the same until the room was scattered with our clothing and we were lying naked together, our chests heaving.

"Your tail is wagging," Tresten pointed out.

"I'm an excited boy," I said.

"Be good and roll over," he said slyly. Then he grabbed me by the arms and flipped me onto my back, straddling me. He lowered his lips to mine, and I felt his warm palm grasp me by the root. Then, after one final kiss, he turned his body around and lowered his mouth to my cock.

Tresten's length hung heavy right in front of my face. I ran my hands slowly over his gorgeous ass cheeks before bringing my tongue along his tip, then up his shaft until I reached his balls. My tongue continued its journey upwards

—and he squirmed slightly, wiggling his ass as I played with his entrance. He moaned over my cock and begged me to stop teasing him.

I pulled his cock back towards my mouth, and happily obeyed his request.

* * *

The next day was the beginning of my training. Before leaving for class, Tresten told me that the first thing he wanted me to do was to sit still. Literally.

"This is one of the first exercises Pa gave me when I was a little kid," he explained. "He forced me to sit completely still for hours, without falling asleep. He told me to think of only one thing—my wolf form. I did this almost every single day before doing any actual physical training."

We'd done meditative exercises in the FAS before, but they were never this intense. If Tresten's father—Pa—used this in his training, then it had to be good. He was one of the most famous living fighters in the world, after all.

I sat cross-legged in the basement training room, trying to keep my mind clear, but it seemed impossible. Unrelenting thoughts of the challenge, of the meeting with our parents, of my arm, of my training, and most of all, of Tresten clouded my head. I glanced at the digital clock on the wall. I'd been sitting for ten minutes, and it'd seemed like I'd been there forever.

"Maybe if I closed my eyes," I mumbled to myself.

I keep the image of my wolf form solid in my thoughts, but it was eroded by everything else. What would my parents think about the challenge? What would Tresten's?

What if I lost?

What was the *real* purpose of this fight? Was honor really worth it?

I remembered what Velvy had told me, that Tresten had done this for me. I understood that. I understood he wanted to help me get payback for what he'd done to me.

But why did he have to put his own future on the line? My honor wasn't worth it. Neither was my training. That was a fucking steep price.

Dammit. Clear mind. Stop thinking.

I opened an eye to peek at the clock. Another ten minutes had passed. I groaned. This was going to be impossible.

TRESTEN

When I got home from class, I found the house dark and quiet. I went to my room to change out of my dirty training clothes. All my moving boxes still sat around unpacked, and I wondered what Loch would think about moving all of my things into the guest bedroom—the one that probably had been meant for us to share. Then I took a quick shower and went to look for Loch.

I peeked into his bedroom. Empty.

Then I tiptoed down to the basement training room and opened the door.

Loch sat in the center, his back facing me, his legs crossed. He didn't react to me entering—had he not moved at all since this morning? *Had he actually managed to clear his mind?* He was sitting so still, so silently—

. . .

The sound of his snore cut off my thoughts.

"Loch!" I shouted.

He bolted awake and spun around, a bit of drool going down the side of his mouth.

"Huh? The hell?"

"You were sleeping!"

"I wasn't sleeping! I wasn't—*fuck*. I was sleeping." He looked up at the clock. "Shit."

I shook my head. "If I were my Pa, you'd be doing a thousand pushups and a thousand shifts. But I'm not going to waste time with that."

"I think I'd rather do a thousand pushups," he yawned. "It'd be easier."

"Your mind is the problem here, not your body." I gave him a kiss. "If we don't get your mind on the same level as your body, you'll lose."

. . .

Loch rubbed his head in frustration. "I've beaten Martin before. Maybe if I train my fighting technique, I can get that slight edge…"

"I don't think so," I said. "I hate to say this, but he does outclass you in strength. And my father always taught me that the best technique starts here." I tapped my head. "The ability to instantly react. To make a judgement call. To not be distracted by his taunts or by anything else that might be nagging on your mind."

"Right." He sighed. "This is not going to be easy."

"No, it's not."

Loch eyed me. "Look, Tresten. Maybe we should rethink this. Fighting Martin is one thing, but to do it with your training on the line? Why are we risking that?"

"You want to back down on Martin?" I asked him. "I'm not going to. I knew what I was doing."

He frowned.

"I just don't know if it's worth it."

. . .

"I think it's worth it, to see him get his ass kicked. To know that he'll never go back to the FAS again. I think that's pretty damn good payback."

"But at the risk of your training."

"It's my training," I said stubbornly.

"And it'll be my fault if you have to resign!"

"You won't lose."

"You don't know that."

"You won't. I have faith in you."

He threw up his hands and walked over to the wall. He rested his forehead against it and closed his eyes. "Fucking hell, Tresten."

I had to do this for him. How else would Loch reach his potential without something to motivate him?

. . .

"Loch," I said gently, touching his back. "I believe in you. I wanted to do this for you. I'm willing to risk everything because I want to see you succeed."

"But why, Tresten?"

"Don't you get it," I said, suddenly feeling self-conscious. "It's because… I really care about you." I looked down at the ground. *No, I've fallen in love with you.* "You're my husband now."

He looked at me with soft eyes and draped his arm over my shoulder. "You're crazy, Tresten." He pulled me into a tight hug. He didn't say anything, but there was something in the way he held me that told me he understood.

We continued mental training for the rest of the day. Loch dozed off once, and by the end, he told me he still didn't feel like anything had changed. I told him that he shouldn't expect anything to change so quickly—it was the first day of training, after all.

Still, a part of me wondered if we had enough time. Loch was stubborn, and mental habits were the hardest to break and reform. I was lucky that I had Desmond Croc for a father. He'd trained me almost since birth, using methods that my grandfather had used to train him. I would need to help Loch re-learn fundamental techniques that I'd practiced over the span of years—and all in two months. Or else… I would have to leave the FAS for good. I could never officially be granted a master ranking.

By the time the weekend arrived, Loch had actually started to see some improvement in his focus.

"I felt it," he told me. "For a whole hour, my mind was blank. It felt like I was floating in the air. I hardly noticed the time go by, but I was tuned in. It was like every one of my senses was electrified, heightened like how they are when I'm shifted."

"Imagine how it'll feel when you *are* shifted," I told him.

We also moved all our things into the spare bedroom, and he helped me finally unpack all of my moving boxes. I hung up my clothes in the closet right next to his, and we brought all of my books on fighting arts, shifter anatomy, and medical techniques out into the living room and stocked the empty shelves with them. Tresten didn't have much—just a small framed family photo that he put up on a dresser in our room, and a cloth scroll with the Crescent Moon Pack's crest on it. He folded that and slid it beneath his pillow.

"Keep this up, and our place might actually start looking like a legitimate home," Loch told me proudly.

. . .

The day of the meeting was a Sunday, and my parents sent a car to pick us up and take us over to the family house. It'd only been a little over a week since I'd moved out—but it felt like I'd been gone for much longer. So much had happened to me in that short time, and I felt like an entirely different person.

I was nervous to be home, but excited to see my parents' reaction to how Loch and I had come together on our own. I could see in his face that Loch was nervous too. He was practically sweating. When my parents greeted us in the foyer, a splash of shock crossed both of their faces as they saw that Loch and I were holding hands. They embraced us both.

"I'm elated for the two of you," Dad said, beaming. "I won't pretend that I wasn't worried for you," he said to me.

"I knew it'd only be a matter of time," Pa said, folding his arms over his chest as he nodded. "Not this fast, but I knew."

"You knew that Loch and I would warm up to each other?" I asked skeptically.

"I did."

"How'd you know, Pa?" Loch asked.

. . .

My heart skipped a beat hearing him call my father Pa.

Pa looked surprised, and then clapped Loch on his good shoulder so hard that I thought he might leave him with two dysfunctional arms. His laugh boomed out through the house. "Oh, this *is* wonderful. Intuition, Loch. Or should I say, *son*."

Loch beamed.

"Pure intuition," Pa continued. "A great fighter needs to have it. You'll develop it, I can tell. Intuition again, see?"

"I didn't believe him," Dad admitted. "We and your parents agreed not to hire help for both of you to force you to work together, in the hope it might bring you together. Honestly, knowing Tresten, I thought it'd only make you hate each other more."

Loch and I exchanged a glance.

"Well, let's get settled," Dad said. "Come in. Loch, your parents should be arriving soon."

William served us my favorite drink and snack—moon tea and grilled cheese sandwiches—and I took Loch on a tour of the house. There was one area that I knew Loch would love: Pa's training room.

The walls of the room were filled with ancient family history. Circling the top of the walls were portraits of the warrior lineage that Pa descended from, going all the way back to my great, great, great, great, great grandfather. There were my grandfather's war medals, photographs from Pa's tournaments and of him schmoozing with all sorts of famous people I didn't know. There was a glass case of Pa's trophies, and above all of them, his certificate of master rank from the FAS.

Loch walked around the room, eyes wide as he took everything in. I thought he'd be most interested in seeing the trophies, but he immediately went over to the aged and weathered wooden dummy in the corner and gave it a reverent touch. "You trained here with Pa?" he asked.

"Almost every day," I said. "I have a lot of memories tied up in this place. Some not so great ones. It was a tough childhood that I've only begun to appreciate now."

He nodded. "I get it. Wow. This place is amazing. There's power here."

"Did you ever train at home with your father? Pa told me that he was one of the best in their class."

. . .

"No, my father spent most of his energy on my two older brothers. The best leadership classes money could buy. Christophe thrived, but I think Arthur never wanted to do any of that shit. Arthur had always been an artist, but you know. Not appropriate for an alpha to do." He rapped the dummy with his fist. "Dad was a great fighter, but he wasn't a great father. Also, we didn't have any of this." He gestured to the portraits of my ancestors. "No fighting lineage to uphold. No ancient training to pass down, or anything like that. Nothing like Pa."

He turned to me. "Do you think it's strange for me to call him 'Pa'? Maybe I should be calling him Master Croc."

I laughed. "No, he liked it. I could tell. He's pleased with himself that he predicted we would get together."

"What do you think about it?"

"I like hearing you call him that, too."

Loch smiled. "I'm glad. But I meant, what do you think about his prediction?"

I blushed. "Oh. Pa does have a way of reading people. But I don't know what he could've seen that would've indicated anything would happen with us."

. . .

"But obviously, there was something there all along," Loch said. He took my hand. "Maybe... we were just meant to be."

William came in to let us know that Loch's parents had just arrived, and we went back to the foyer with my parents to greet them. Loch straightened when his parents entered. He hugged his mother and gave a stiff bow to his father.

"When will your shoulder be functional?" he asked gruffly.

"It's healing," Loch answered. "Another week, maybe two."

"This never should have happened in the first place," his mother said. "Whoever did this to you should be punished."

"Well," I said, "that's part of what we want to discuss today. Among... other things."

"Why don't we take this to the sitting room," Dad suggested. "There are refreshments."

The sitting room had a circle of plush sofas and armchairs arranged next to a large fireplace, over which hung an oil painting of my great great great grandmother, standing strongly on a majestic cliff with her wolf form sitting next to her. Loch and I took a seat next to each other on one of the sofas, and his parents looked at us with obvious surprise.

They both looked to my parents for confirmation of what they were seeing. Pa and Dad just smiled.

"Tresten and I have… developed feelings for each other," Loch announced, very officially.

Pa, who was sitting in an armchair next to Loch's father, reached over and socked him on the arm. "Told you, Basch. You owe me money."

"And I'll gladly pay it," Loch's father replied. "This is excellent news."

"A sure shock," his mother agreed. "Does this mean that the two of you have already… fulfilled the second part of the contract?"

The second part of the contract...

It took me a moment to remember what that even was. I'd gotten so swept up in everything that'd happened that I'd completely forgotten about the most important part of this whole arrangement—the entire reason why I was even married to Loch.

My parents looked at us eagerly, waiting for our response.

. . .

"No," Loch said, and he snuck his hand into mine. "Not yet."

"Then, soon?" Dad asked.

"Well," said Loch. "I don't know."

"I would hope it will be soon," said Loch's father. "Especially if it need not be forced now. It's even more reason for you both to go through with it immediately. Why wait?"

"That's right," said Pa.

Loch looked at me questioningly, like he was waiting for my agreement.

"I don't know…"

"Tresten," Dad said, "I know you realize that your child is the reason for this agreement. Our family is still in a precarious position…"

"We have the backing of the Lunas now," I said.

"Backing if our family is challenged," Dad said.

· · ·

"It would be hazardous to let it get to that point," Loch's mother said.

"Loch?" his father said. "It's your responsibility to fill."

Loch looked at me. "Tresten and I will discuss it privately," he said. "We have other things we need to talk with you about. There's something pretty urgent that we need to discuss."

I was relieved that Loch had diverted the subject. *A baby*. The thought of having a child with Loch brought such warmth to my heart. There would've been no question in my mind, no hesitation, if it weren't for all of the things that were confronting me right now—the fight, the training, my future…

Our parents all started to talk at once.

His mother frowned. "What could be more urgent than the baby?"

Pa looked annoyed. "You can't just disregard this responsibility, Tresten."

"That's right."

. . .

"...Family depends on it..."

"You two *need* to settle it as soon as possible. Do you need aphrodisiacs? We can order them from the tiger clans—"

I raised my voice to cut through the noise. "Loch and I have issued an official fight challenge to a member of the Blood Gulch Clan."

The room went dead silent.

"You did what?" Loch's mother said.

"A challenge?" Pa asked, leaning forward in his chair. "Who?"

"Martin Bellock," Loch answered. "He was responsible for this wound. I'm going to fight him in two months. Tresten is going to help train me."

A murmur.

"An official challenge seems a little extreme for that," Pa said. "This is something that could be settled in class. It's an accepted risk of training. You both should understand that."

. . .

"He insulted Tresten," Loch said. "I won't repeat what he said, but he disrespected him in front of me. He disrespected Vander as well, and our whole family."

"A challenge brings our clans into this," Loch's mother said sternly. "This is not something to be taken lightly."

"It wasn't," I said. "I can assure you of that, Mother." She looked at me with a raised eyebrow, but then seemed to look pleased that I'd called her that.

"What are the terms?" Dad asked.

I took a deep breath. "That if Martin Bellock loses, he will permanently resign from the FAS."

"And if Loch loses?"

"Then… I will permanently resign."

"What?!" Pa shouted.

Dad's mouth dropped. "Tresten!"

. . .

I had not expected that reaction from them. In fact, the reaction between our parents was the complete opposite of what I expected. Loch's parents sat quietly, contemplating. My parents were outraged. Loch gave me a nervous glance.

"How can we agree to enforce those terms over something so minor?" Pa bellowed.

"I agree that the cause for the challenge is something that probably should've been addressed quietly," Loch's mother said. "However, I'd love nothing more than to have those Blood Gulch upstarts learn their place. Vander has complained that he's been bullied by their members in school before."

"I agree with Desmond," said Loch's father. "This was irresponsible."

"Dad," Loch protested. "Isn't it an alpha's duty to protect the name of his family and his mate? Didn't you teach me that?"

His father deflated, grumbling.

"We'll need to speak with other clan members about this," Pa said. "The challenge is set, that can't be changed. But I don't know if the Ice River Pack will be able to enforce the terms. It may end up depending on honor—yours, and this Martin Bellock's."

LOCH

"I thought they'd back us up," Tresten said dejectedly.

Back at home from the family meeting, Tresten and I sat in the middle of the basement training room, neither one of us able to concentrate on exercises.

"I was too hasty," he said. "And here I've been lecturing you about not letting your emotions take over your actions, and I got us into this mess."

I took his hands into mine and kissed them, hoping to give him some reassurance. "If the clans aren't going to enforce the terms, Martin will say fuck off to resigning. Which means there's nothing holding you to it, either."

. . .

"You know that they'd slander us if we lost and didn't uphold the terms, though. You know they have zero honor."

He was right. The Blood Gulch Clan and the Bellock family were filled with scumbag pieces of dog shit just like Martin. They'd no doubt avoid the punishment if the Ice River and Crescent Moons refused to use their elder status to enforce the terms.

"Loch," Tresten said, looking at me with worried eyes. "I think… I think I messed up."

I smiled and wrapped my arms around him. "You did what you thought was right. There's nothing wrong with that."

"Yeah, but… I shouldn't have put you on the line like that, it wasn't fair for you. I was cocky and acted on impulse."

"You're being too hard on yourself," I said. "And there's nothing wrong with trusting your gut. You know that. Don't blame yourself. If it weren't for you, I probably would've gotten myself in even more trouble."

Tresten's head hung low. I'd never seen him look so dispirited before.

. . .

"I feel ashamed of myself. I'm so sorry, Loch. I thought I was thinking about you and doing something good for us, but it was a mistake." He buried his face into my arm. "I'm sorry. I'm sorry."

"You have nothing to be sorry for," I told him. My heart ached to see him this hurt. "You have no idea how proud I was when you challenged him like you did. I mean, how badass was that? You were amazing."

"I just couldn't let him get away with that shit anymore."

"I know. And that's why I love you."

The words had just slipped out of my mouth.

Tresten looked at me, his eyes wide. Then he smiled—no, more like *beamed*. "I love you too, Loch."

We kissed, and the fireworks erupted in my head just like it was the first time. I wrapped my arms around him, slowly lowering him to the floor. His hands caressed my cheeks, his eyes like glimmering sapphires as he gazed deeply into mine. Everything seemed to melt away around us.

"What have you done to me?" I murmured to him. "I love you so much."

"Loch…"

Our kisses grew more passionate, and our touch more desperate. I ached for him. Tresten pulled my shirt from my body and tossed it across the room, and immediately went for the knot at my waist. My pants joined my shirt in a crumpled heap against the wall. When I'd wrestled Tresten's shirt free, I kissed and nipped at his neck, moving lower across his perfect pecs and rippling abs. My cock throbbed sorely, tenting up my underwear, and Tresten's palm moved down to meet it. His eager fingertips slipped beneath the waistband and took hold of my length, and he pulled me closer to him.

"Will you take me?" he whispered.

My heart and head whirled. "Are you sure?"

"I want it."

Everything in my mind vanished except for one burning, pulsing thought. I could feel my alpha wolf howling inside for Tresten's omega, and it had one primal goal.

We wrestled his pants from his hips, and then drew down his underwear so that his cock sprung free. Tresten, with all his toughness and strength, looked vulnerable now. He looked at me with a nervous expectancy shining in his eyes. "I love you," I told him, and then lowered myself down to kiss him again. Our cocks slid against one another as our bodies met, and I reached down and used my hand to squeeze them together. I could feel the wetness from the tip of his cock mixing with my precome, slickening our lengths. I could smell his delicious scent strongly in the air—he was ready for me.

I pushed his thighs up and back so that his knees were at his shoulders. His cock rested back on his stomach, covering his belly button. I brought one finger down and slowly slid it inside him. He was wet with his omega lust, and it entered him easily. Tresten's forehead crinkled and a gasp escaped his lips.

"Is that okay?" I asked gently.

"Yes."

Then I slipped a second finger in, and began to slowly move them in and out. I could feel him loosening, the tension slowly going away.

"That feels good," he moaned.

Next, I used my free hand to stroke his cock as I fingered him. I loved feeling his reactions around my fingers, telling me exactly what movement he liked the best. I picked up speed, and his mouth dropped open into a silent O, his eyes locked with mine in an amazed expression that read, "How does this feel so good?"

I grinned. I loved seeing his pleasure and knowing that I was the one who was giving it to him. This was Tresten's first time—and mine too, with an omega. More than that, it was the first time with my husband, the man I'd fallen in love with. I was going to savor it, and make sure he enjoyed every single moment.

"Give me the real thing," he said, reaching down between my legs and tugging me. "I can take it."

"Okay," I said. My heart was thundering in my chest. "Let me get a condom."

"Fuck the condom. You're my mate."

"Are you sure?" I asked.

"Are you?"

He didn't need to ask. "Yes. Of course."

. . .

I took hold of the base of my cock and positioned it with my thumb and forefinger at his opening. A nervous and excited tremble shook my whole body. Then I slowly entered him. Tresten cried out, and his hands grabbed my wrists and held on tight as I pushed forward. A low groan slipped from my lips as I plunged into absolute blissful pleasure. *He was so tight* —it felt like we were corresponding puzzle pieces made perfectly for each other. I was in danger of exploding right on the first thrust.

Clear your mind, hold it together.

Calling on everything I'd learned over the last week's training, I was able to hold on.

"Oh, shit," Tresten moaned. "Oh, *shit...* You're inside me…"

My hips started to move, and Tresten threw his arms around my neck and pulled my lips to his. "It feels so good," he said. "Does it feel good for you, Loch?"

"The best," I managed.

"Does it feel good being inside me?"

I nodded, gritting my teeth. "Fuck, it feels so good. It doesn't…hurt you…?" I was doing everything I could just to hold it together.

Tresten shook his head. "I can deal with the pain. I like it."

I thrust in harder and faster until the walls were echoing with the sound of our lovemaking, and my cock reached as deep into Tresten as it could go. It felt like every time I pushed in, his tightness would grip at me, almost begging me not to withdraw from him. He reached down and started to stroke himself in rhythm with my movements.

It was more than I could handle. "Tresten," I grunted, "I'm going to come."

"Do it inside of me," he begged me, and he wrapped his legs around my waist.

I felt my cock knot up deep inside him when the orgasm exploded over me, and I shouted his name. Tresten tossed his head back, and I felt him tighten around me. He hit his climax at the exact same time as me, and his come shot up onto his chest. I slammed in one last time, my cock throbbing out and filling him up with everything I had.

* * *

Tresten and I laid together for a long time in the middle of the training room floor, naked in each other's arms and just enjoying the feeling of each other. I'd never felt so content in my life. I felt whole.

A little over a week ago, I'd had little expectations for my future. That had been the outlook I was born into. I was the third alpha, and so I would always be the least important member of my family. Marrying Tresten had given me some purpose, a way to please my parents and do service to my family, but it'd confirmed for me that I'd never have any real contentment for myself. I was destined to be trapped with someone I didn't like. Someone who hated me.

How wrong could I have been?

He was my mate. My fated mate.

I pulled Tresten against me even tighter, and kissed his forehead. He smiled and rested his cheek on my chest. "I love you," I said. "My mate."

He laughed. "That sounds so funny coming from you."

"Hey."

"I never could've imagined *the* Loch Luna calling anyone his mate. Let alone me." He kissed my chest, right below my collar bone. "I love it."

. . .

"Don't tell anyone at the FAS," I said. "I've got a reputation to keep."

"Too late for that. Everyone knows we're married, now."

"At least now I don't have to bite my tongue when those horn dogs check you out," I said.

"Were you jealous?"

"More like annoyed. I told you. Nobody touches my husband except me."

He circled his fingertips around my chest and gave my nipple a little pinch. "So protective."

We gave up on trying to do anymore training that night. All we wanted to do was be together, enjoying each other. We went upstairs and took a long shower together, and afterwards, cuddled up together in bed. Tresten fell asleep almost immediately. He looked so peaceful. There was none of his usual intensity in his sleeping face. I listened to the sound of his breathing until it carried me off into what was the best sleep of my life.

TRESTEN

It took Loch's arm two weeks to heal, and by two weeks after the meeting with my parents we were back to doing full physical exercises alongside the mental training. Loch, of course, had hardly any problems with the physical training. He bounced right back, almost as if nothing had happened to begin with. If fact, he was so eager to use both arms again I had to warn him to keep himself together or else risk hurting himself. The mental training was not so good. He had made a lot of progress compared to when he'd first started, but his shifts were still slow and his decisions still too clouded.

Loch was finally able to come back and train in class, and it seemed like the challenge was on the minds of everyone, even Master Graffer. He stopped pairing Martin with me or Loch during training, and would quietly drop Loch little extra nuggets of advice.

. . .

I'd never seen him train so seriously before. It was constant—meditation and concentration exercises from the moment he got out of bed, Master Graffer's training in class, and then more sparring and mental training with me when we got home—and course a little extra physical training in the bedroom before we slept.

"Is that your fastest? Come on, Loch!"

He came at me, jaws snapping, and I effortlessly sailed over him and nipped his nail with my teeth. He spun around and came at me again, this time landing a closer blow. "Almost," he grunted. "You're just too fast, Tresten. You always have been."

"Dog shit. You know I'm slower now than I ever was."

"But still faster than most," he panted, his tongue hanging out the side of his mouth. We both shifted back to human form, and I tossed him a towel. "I feel like things are getting clearer, but I just can't reach this level of calm you're talking about. How do I even know it exists? Maybe I've already reached my limit. You'd had training from birth, after all." He wiped his face and the sweat dripping down his chest.

"It's going to be harder for you. But I refuse to believe that you're at your limit. We need to keep trying. After all, you'll be facing an entirely different challenge during the real match. We should assume that Martin fuckface isn't going to fight straight."

Loch laughed. "'Martin fuckface. Yeah, I know." He kissed my cheek. "I love you."

"I love you too," I smiled. "Work on your meditations. I'm going to go take a shower and get dinner ready. Velvy is coming over to eat with us."

"Let me know if you need any help," he said.

"I can handle it. I think I've gotten pretty good at cooking."

He gave me a cheeky grin. "I wasn't talking about the cooking."

I snorted and punched his chest. "Shut up and meditate."

Having Loch give me a helping hand in the shower sounded like a fantastic idea, but every spare moment we had was precious and needed to be dedicated to training. There was less than a month until the fight.

I stepped into the shower and started to lather up my hair with shampoo.

. . .

Was I afraid that Loch would lose? I would be lying if I said that I wasn't. I wanted to have complete faith in him—after all, I loved him. I'd learned that Loch was the type of person who would have faith in anything I did, so why was it that I was so worried that he could do this? Why did I feel like he wasn't ready? Loch was strong. He could easily destroy most of the others in our class. But I could tell that Loch still had a chink in his armor, a weakness that could be exploited by someone like Martin.

I needed to have faith in him. I needed to believe that he wouldn't let me down.

Or else, I needed to prepare myself for the reality that I might actually need to resign from the FAS.

I ran my hands through my hair and let the water rinse out the shampoo. When I dropped my hand down, I froze at what I saw on my palm.

What...?

Streaks of black hair clumped in my hand. I looked down at the clouds of shampoo floating toward the drain and saw the lines of black hair going along with them.

. . .

"Oh, shit," I coughed.

I burst out of the shower and ran to the mirror. My mark was gone. My hair was completely white again; the black streak had fallen out.

"Loch… LOCH!" I ran out naked, still dripping water and shampoo. "LOCH!"

He burst out of the basement and caught me in the hallway. "What's wrong?!" he shouted, grabbing my shoulders. "What is it? What happened?"

I held out my palm, the loose black hair still sitting in it. "Look," I breathed.

"What is that?" His eyes widened when the realization hit him. "Oh, shit. Oh, *shit*. What does that mean? Does that mean what I think it means?"

"I don't know," I said.

"You don't know? Didn't you have omega education or something? How do you not know?"

. . .

"I never paid attention! I didn't give a damn about any of that back then."

"What do we do?"

"I don't know!" I stared at the hair in my palm and held it out in front of me like a gigantic wasp had landed on my hand. "We'll ask Velvy. She'll know."

I quickly finished up in the shower. Loch sat on the couch in the living room, his chin in his palm and his eyes wide as an owl's. I sat next to him, and he put his arm around my shoulder. We both seemed to be avoiding mentioning the word that was on our minds.

"We'll be okay," he said, finally. "Things are going to be okay for us."

I nodded.

Loch squeezed my leg. "Let's make dinner."

The two of us went to the kitchen together and set to work making a batch of spaghetti and meatballs. The routine of cooking quickly helped to dull the nervous edge we both were feeling, and again I was reminded of just how amazingly lucky I was to be with Loch. We were a team. No matter what happened, we were together and had each other's backs. I realized, at that moment, that the future *was* really going to be okay. It didn't matter if I had to leave the FAS. *Nothing* mattered—as long as we were together, everything would be just fine.

When Velvy knocked on the door, the noodles were steaming in the pot ready to be served, and the house was filled with the savory-sweet aroma of tomato sauce. The two of us hurried to go answer it and let her in.

"I brought some wine," she said. "I hope you—hounds of Hell! Tresten!" She nearly dropped the bag she was holding and pointed at my hair. Loch and I exchanged a glance.

"Come in, Velvy," I said.

She put the bag with the wine bottles onto the counter and pulled one out. "Well, Tresten, I guess you won't be having any wine, then."

"So… it does mean?"

She looked at me and laughed. "You didn't know? I guess I should've known that. Congratulations, you two. Tresten, you aren't in heat anymore. You guys are going to have a baby!"

. . .

I felt dizzy, like the world around me had suddenly exploded in size, leaving me whirling helplessly in the center of it all. *I'm pregnant.* Fear, worry, confusion, and wonder all shot through me before being replaced with blissful happiness. *I'm pregnant. Loch and I are going to have a baby.*

I turned to Loch and saw tears welling up in his eyes. He pulled me into a tight hug. "I love you," he said. "I can't believe it. This is incredible."

Velvy popped open the wine bottle and poured two glasses out, and a third glass of orange juice for me. "I mean, you guys did have sex. You guys *did* know what sex does, right?"

"Yeah," I said, laughing as I wiped away tears. "But I don't think either of us had thought about it after the fact… it just kind of happened. Again, and again, and again."

"You guys are adorable," Velvy said, handing Loch the glass of wine. "Cheers to you guys, the most unlikely couple I'll probably ever know."

We clinked glasses, and I sipped the orange juice. "Thanks, Velvy."

"The most unlikely *family*, now," Loch marveled. "Shit, what will our parents say? I don't think even Pa would've predicted this would happen so soon."

. . .

"I don't think so either," I said. "None of them will have expected this."

We sat down and enjoyed dinner together, talking and laughing. I suddenly had a vision of the future—of Loch and I together, and our child. Having dinners like this, with friends and family, our children running around the house. I remembered back to when I was a child, and all the things my parents had showed me. *I'm pregnant.* Soon, Loch and I would show our own child the way.

At that moment, nothing else mattered. The training, the fight, the FAS, my future as a fighter. Having a child had never been my priority in life. In fact, the idea used to terrify me. But now?

Suddenly, I could feel a spot of warmth in my belly, glowing like a sun. I rested my hands on my stomach. *Who will you be?* I couldn't wait to find out.

The tears started to flow without warning. I lowered my head, trying to hide them, but soon I was weeping openly.

"Tresten? What's the matter?" Loch turned from his conversation with Velvy and put his arms around me, leaning close.

. . .

"What is it, Tresten?" Velvy asked, worried.

"I'm sorry," I hiccupped through my tears. "I'm just... so happy."

LOCH

There was only two weeks until the fight, and I still felt off. It seemed like I'd actually started to regress with my training. I was getting slower. My attacks were more distracted. I'd nearly reinjured my shoulder after I lost my footing landing a leaping strike.

Our parents were ecstatic to learn that Tresten and I were expecting, of course, and I was too—but I found my mind drawn to the future and away from the present moment, where it needed to be to fight at its full potential. I was thinking about Tresten and what this pregnancy would mean for him. I was thinking about our child. This fight had grown further away from me now more than ever, to the point where I almost couldn't remember why I was doing it. Why was I risking my neck for this? My husband was pregnant.

What kind of father would I be? Would I even be any good as a dad? It wasn't a question I'd even thought to consider at any other time in my life, and now, suddenly, here it was. This new reality.

To celebrate our happy marriage, our pregnancy, and the official joining of our clans and families, our parents insisted on throwing a clan dinner party. Tresten and I both tried to get out of it, but in the end had to agree out of duty. Even with limited time before the fight, we were required to take a day off to schmooze and introduce ourselves to each other's relatives.

A buzzer went off, indicating the end of our hour meditation exercise. It was the day of the party, but I was going to keep training as long as I could before we had to head out. I opened my eyes and sighed. Tresten was sitting cross-legged next to me. He looked over.

"What is it?"

I laid back on the floor and spread my arms out. The long fluorescent lights above me burnt white bars into my vision that swam around when I shut my eyes. I felt Tresten's hand sneak into mine. "What?" he asked again.

"I haven't been improving," I said. "I think I'm getting worse. I can't clear my mind. The exercises aren't working how they were. I can't stop thinking about… our child. About you. About how this might be a terrible idea."

. . .

"We've been over this, Loch."

"I know, but things are different now, aren't they? What if I don't win?"

"Then… I leave the FAS. Simple as that."

I looked at him.

"I'm going to have to, anyway," he said. "I'll need to take a break to raise our child. I already need to cut down on training. That's just the reality of it. I accepted this."

"It must be so hard for you," I said. "I wish you didn't have to choose."

He shook his head. "In the end, it wasn't. It was what I needed to do." He exhaled and leaned back on his arms. He tilted his head back, like he was looking up at the sky through the ceiling and our home above us. His gorgeous milk-white hair fell across his forehead. His eyes shone clean like blue water with a peaceful confidence I wasn't sure I'd seen before. He looked radiant. "I believe in you, Loch. You don't need to worry."

I smiled and wished that I felt the same way. I wasn't ready for this fight. My head was not in it.

. . .

Tresten rolled over and nuzzled his head into my chest. "I love you, Loch," he said.

"I love you too, Tresten."

"What are you hoping the baby will be?" he asked. "A girl or a boy?"

I paused, pretending to think about it. Of course, it was something I'd already thought about before. "A boy," I said. "A strong little omega, like you."

Tresten chuckled. "Really?"

"Yeah. We could both teach him how to fight, if he showed the talent and interest."

"He's our son. Of course, he would."

"What are you hoping the baby will be?" I asked.

"A boy," Tresten said. "I wouldn't have the slightest idea of what to do with a girl. But... I don't know about him being an omega."

. . .

"Why not?"

"It's hard to be an omega."

"That didn't stop you from kicking ass," I said.

"I just don't know if I'd want that life for my child. My life was never easy."

I thought about that for a moment. "No. But great people and great things are born from hardship. Like you."

"Getting philosophical?"

I smiled. "It's true. At least, I think it is. But I do know for certain that you're one of the most amazing people I've ever known, Tresten."

He looked up at me, and I saw pure happiness in his eyes that I knew was reflected back in mine. I held him tight and kissed him, and felt the fireworks exploding in my head. "Do you feel that?" I asked him.

"Feel what?"

. . .

"The fireworks when we kiss."

"Every single time."

We lay on the floor of the training room for a while longer, enjoying the moment in the place where so many of our good moments had been shared.

"We'd better get ready for this dinner," I said.

Tresten groaned. "Do we have to? I hate these official dinners."

"Really?" I asked, helping him to his feet. "What's not to like? All the small talk, the annoying relatives and clan members whose names you can never remember… and of course, all the alcohol you can drink. Or maybe that's what makes these things bearable."

"I can't drink," Tresten reminded me.

"Ooh. Ouch. This *is* going to be a pain in the ass for you, then. Don't mind while I get wasted."

. . .

He laughed and punched my arm. "Hey. This isn't any ordinary party, remember? Every eye is going to be on us."

"I'll keep it together," I promised. "But I'm going to need a few drinks to keep it together."

We went up to our room and dug into the closet for our formal clothing. I held mine up and gave it a contemptuous look. "I haven't worn this thing since the Dawn Academy entrance ceremony."

"At least yours is just a normal dress suit. I have this monstrosity." He held up the set of traditional omega robes he'd been wearing at our wedding officiation.

"I like those on you," I admitted.

"They're horrible. It's got a fucking *bow* on the back, Loch. A bow."

"I thought it made you look adorable at our wedding."

"Thanks? I don't know if I want to look adorable." He sighed. "Help me tie this thing on?"

. . .

I helped with the robes layers and with the despised bow. I kept it to myself, but I thought he looked even more adorable than he had the first time I'd seen him in it. After I was done assisting him, Tresten helped me tie my tie. He pushed the knot up to my neck and adjusted it to center.

"You look hot," he said, and looked away.

I laughed and kissed him. "This kind of feels like we're going to our own wedding again."

A car arrived to pick the two of us up, and with Tresten by my side, I was surprised to find myself getting excited about our first official event together as husbands.

* * *

The Croc home had been dressed up in a spectacular party display. The front driveway was filled with luxury cars, with a valet service greeting and parking arriving guests under an awning of twinkling lights draped between two huge wolf sculptures. One, representing the Ice River Clan, was carved entirely out of ice. The other, for the Crescent Moons, was made of polished marble. The front doors were pulled open, and I could see the crowd of party guests mingling inside. The driver brought our car past the valet and into the private garage attached to the house so that Tresten and I could arrive discreetly and make our entrance.

William, the Croc butler, greeted us in the garage.

. . .

"Your parents are entertaining the guests," he informed us. "Trying to keep things orderly."

"Is everything okay?" I asked. There were bound to be members on both sides who still felt the tensions from our feuding days, so I worried about the possibility that there might be some unpleasant encounters, especially when the alcohol had been flowing for a while.

"Some of the Crescent Moon members seem to be feeling rather isolated," William said. "Mr. and Mr. Croc have been doing their best. But it's good you've both arrived."

"My parents aren't here yet?" I asked, surprised. "What about my brothers?"

"Not yet arrived," William said. "I've attempted to contact them, but there was no response."

"Huh." I checked my cell phone—no missed calls, no missed messages. "Okay. I'm sure they'll be here soon."

Great, now I would have to do diplomatic work. That was Christophe's forte, not mine.

. . .

We followed William until we reached the door leading out into the back, and I could hear the music and chatter from the party Tresten took my hand, and William opened the door for us.

It seemed like the entire gathering turned around to look at us at the same time, and then broke out into warm applause. As we walked through the parting crowd, Tresten and I smiled and shook hands with our well-wishers until we finally reached Dad and Pa Croc.

"Any idea where your parents are?" Pa said privately to me.

"They must just be running late," I said. "I haven't heard anything from them."

He nodded and patted me on the shoulder before turning to address the guests. *Where were my parents and my brothers?* It was unusual for them to be late, and at the least, I would've expected Christophe to have contacted me with an update. I checked my phone again. Nothing.

Tresten looped his arm through mine and gave me a quick, questioning look. I shrugged.

"Thank you all for coming," Pa said. "Distinguished families of both the Crescent Moon and Ice River Clans. Tonight, we're here to celebrate the bonding of Tresten Croc and

Loch Luna—and the announcement of their first child." There were some surprised and delighted murmurs as everyone broke out into loud applause. "And of course, the joining of our clans, once divided for generations, now allied in friendship. The Ice River Clan will pledge to be at the side of the Crescent Moons, joined as family, to protect their interests and their kin as our own."

Pa looked at me and smiled, and I realized this was where Dad would've stepped in to complete the speech. *Where the hell were they?* I stepped forward nervously. I was not a public speaker. "The Crescent Moon Clan returns that promise," I said quickly, nearly stumbling over my words. Tresten squeezed my arm. "Thank you all so much for being here."

Everyone cheered and applauded.

"Let's have a toast," Dad Croc said, lifting his glass. A flute of champagne was passed over to me, and one of sparkling cider for Tresten. The crowd raised their glasses, which shimmered under the twinkling overhead lights. "To the future of our families."

I saw William hurrying through the side of the crowd to where we were. There was something about the look on his face that sent a strange feeling into my stomach. He tapped Pa on the shoulder and whispered something in his ear. Pa frowned and stepped aside. I watched as William spoke briskly into his ear. Pa's eyes widened in a look of shock.

. . .

"What is it?" I asked, forgetting about the crowd that was waiting for us to finish the toast.

Pa came over and grabbed my arm. He spoke low in my ear. "There's been an incident. Your brother, Vander. He was badly hurt by one of his classmates—a Bellock boy. Your parents are in the hospital with him."

"I need to go!" I shouted. "I need to go to the hospital!"

There was a murmur from the crowd.

Tresten had overheard Pa. "That fucking *scum*." He grabbed my arm and pulled me with him through the crowd. Confused eyes followed us.

"My friends," I heard Pa say, his voice booming out. "Please listen. There's been an incident…"

I was reeling. *They'll pay for this. Those bastards will pay for this.*

TRESTEN

A phone call from Loch's parents came through while we were already speeding towards the hospital. They were there with Van. He was fine and awake, but had suffered severe injuries to his leg, and it was uncertain if it would fully heal.

One of Martin Bellock's younger brothers had berated him into a fight, and several of the little brat's friends ganged up on him. I was livid, burning with anger, and I could see that Loch was barely holding it together. I kept his hand tight in mine, trying to be strong for him, to keep him centered. He stared straight ahead at nothing, his eyes flashing with both shock and fury.

We screeched up to the front of the hospital and found Loch's older brother Arthur waiting outside for us. He greeted us with a hug and ushered us inside to follow him.

. . .

"Van is fine," he said. "He's pissed off at himself."

"How's his leg?" Loch asked as we rushed through the hospital.

"They're going to need to operate. It's badly broken."

"Fucking *shit*," Loch growled. We passed some nurses who gave him a look.

"Will it be okay?" I asked.

"They don't know."

"How's he taking it?" Loch asked.

Arthur stopped in front of a door. "You can ask him yourself." He opened it, and we went inside.

Mom and Dad stood up and came over to us, wrapping us both into unusually tight and warm hugs.

"Mom, Dad…" Loch said.

. . .

Christophe came up and hugged us both next.

We walked into the room and saw a very bruised up Van lying in the hospital bed. He gave us a weak smile. "Hey, guys. Sorry I messed up the party. I really screwed up."

Loch came to his bedside. "No way, Van. No way. I'm proud of you. Standing up to those shit heads."

"They said you'd lose, Loch," Van said. Tears started to well up and pour down his swollen cheeks. "They kept saying you were weak. That you… had no balls because you were an omega—" He paused and looked over at Mom before lowering his voice. "An omega fucker. And that Martin was going to kill you."

I put my hand on Loch's back, knowing the stir of rage he must've felt at that moment. I had to do everything I could to quiet it in myself.

"No," Loch said, shaking his head. "Don't worry about that, little bro. I'm going to take care of that joke of an alpha, no problem. He's not going to get away with this."

"I think my leg is done," Van said plainly.

. . .

"Don't say that," Mom said.

"Yeah," said Loch. "They're going to operate."

"I know the doctors are just trying to sound optimistic," Van said. "I'm not an idiot. I can hear it in their voices. I know it's fucked."

Mom flinched at the curse, but said nothing. Just then, there was a knock on the door. Christophe got up and opened it.

"Mr. Croc," he said, surprised. My Pa was standing in the doorway.

"I came as quickly as I could," Pa said. "Julius is still at the house, tending to the guests."

"Thank you for coming, Desmond," said Dad Luna, shaking Pa's hand. Mom gave him a hug. "It seems we have more to add to our plate concerning these damn Blood Gulch Bellocks."

Pa nodded. "Yes. I took the liberty of speaking to the other members of the Ice River and Crescent Moons. With everyone gathered in one place it was easy to make them aware of the entire situation. Needless to say—the challenge has the official backing and enforcement of both packs now.

They've injured two of ours, one seriously. This will *not* be forgiven."

Loch and I exchanged a glance, and I could immediately see the change that was in his eyes. *Loch was ready to fight*.

We spent an hour at the hospital before Van was given medication to help him sleep through the pain. The operation would be the following day.

Back at home, Loch and I silently moved to the bedroom to change out of our dress clothes. Loch was checked out, his focus somewhere distant. His eyes were tense and fierce, and I knew he was thinking about the fight. He yanked off his tie and tossed it on the ground.

I came over to him and helped him remove his jacket, sliding it back on its hanger. "Remember your training," I told him, stroking his arm. "It's the only way you'll get through this."

"Hm," he grunted. "I know I'm going to destroy him. I'm going to get that fuck and smash him into the ground. I'm going to get him back for everything he's done. He's not going to last one second."

"Loch," I said evenly. "Listen to me." I took his face in my hands. "Look at me."

. . .

His fiery eyes met mine.

"Remember your training," I repeated. "You're slipping." I let my hands fall to his shoulders, and then his biceps. I could feel him shaking. I could see the rage in his face.

"I'm trying," he said. "But I feel like I'm about to explode. How dare they. How *dare* they."

"I know," I said softly. "But you need to keep present. You need to keep your mind balanced." I leaned forward and kissed his lips. "You can do this."

"I'm so angry," he murmured, and shut his eyes. "Dammit, Tresten. Those *fuckers*…"

"I know," I repeated, my voice low. I kissed him again. "I love you, Loch."

"I love you too," he said.

He kissed me back, and I felt his body relaxing some. I ran my fingers through his hair and down his neck. Our kiss turned deeper, and our tongues moved into each other's mouths, probing hungrily. *Center yourself, Loch*, I thought. *Don't let it build up.*

. . .

I let my hands move down his chest.

Let me help you.

His lips moved to my neck, kissing and sucking me to almost the point of pain. I couldn't restrain a moan. Then I felt his hands go down to my waist, pulling me tight against him.

Use me. Let me relieve you.

I slipped my hand beneath the band of his pants and felt his waiting hardness. He groaned, and then grabbed me around my waist and turned me around. He pushed me against the wall and yanked the bow that held my robes together free, pushing them open so that I was immediately exposed.

"Yeah," I murmured. "Loch…" I pushed my rear out towards him, presenting myself for him.

I heard the jangle of his belt and the thump of his pants hitting the floor. His hand pressed against the back of my neck.

"Shift your tail," he commanded. "I want to see your tail out."

. . .

I didn't question him or say a word. I closed my eyes and let my tail shift out from its place right above my crack. I was so hard, and I could feel the warm wetness in my opening, ready for him.

He grabbed me by the tail and pulled it up. I gasped in surprise, and then spread my legs for him. He pressed up against me. I didn't hold back my moan as he entered me.

There was nothing gentle about this. The house shook as Loch fucked me, pulling my tail as he slammed deep inside my ass, my face pressed up against the wall. I realized I was drooling, it felt so fucking good. My eyes rolled back as I felt his entire rock hard cock burying all the way into me.

Let it all out.

His strained grunts reminded me of how he sounded when he fought. It only turned me on more. I moaned and screamed as I got slammed from behind, until my legs nearly gave out as an orgasm exploded over me, almost out of nowhere. My cock throbbed as I came, pulsing out against the wall. Then Loch hit climax. I felt him stretch me out even more as his cock swelled up and knotted with his finish. He slammed the wall with his forearm, growling out a shout of ecstasy as I felt all his tension and frustration leave his body. I could feel the hotness filling me up, spilling deep inside of me. I loved every moment of it.

. . .

When we collapsed into bed in each other's arms, Loch's eyes were normal again. He wrapped me up into a tight hug, and covered me with kisses. "I love you so much," he told me.

"I love you too," I said, nuzzling against his chest.

LOCH

Two days before the fight, a bank of dark clouds invaded the sky and the smell of coming rain filled the air. I skipped my lessons at the FAS for the final day to stay at home and try to keep my mind clear and focused.

I'd like to say that after the two months of training, I'd pulled through and mastered my mind—but that just wouldn't be true. I'd made improvements, but there were times when I felt like nothing had changed at all. Thoughts were constantly in the back of my mind, of Tresten, of our child, of my pack—and now of Van. The surgery had been a success, but the damage done would leave his leg weaker and vulnerable to injury. Van's dream was to become a fighter. He already had the handicap of being an omega, and now he had to deal with his leg. He'd put on a strong face, but I knew he was torn up inside about it—and I was too. Rage burned inside me every time I thought about it, and it was so hard to clear it from my head.

. . .

Tresten was doing his best to keep me centered, but I knew that his mind was also in other places. I could tell that he was still struggling with the fact that he might never train again. He'd told me he'd accepted it, but I knew him. I knew how much it meant to him. Occasionally, I'd see a certain look cross over his face and I knew his mind was off somewhere far.

The night before the fight, the sky opened up and poured rain across the city. Tresten had started to feel sick from the pregnancy, and called Velvy to come over to keep him company while I isolated myself down in the basement. I knew trying to sleep would be a waste of time, so I decided to try and meditate through the night. My mind would not go clear. It seemed like every single thought and memory was bombarding my head at the same time. I thought of my first days at the FAS. I thought of my father, telling me I shouldn't ever expect to be a great fighter. I thought of the first time I remembered seeing Tresten in school, and how insignificant he was to me then. I thought of everything that had happened over the past two months with him. I thought of our child.

I knew there was a chance that I could be seriously injured or even killed in this fight. It was an official match and so the rules of civilized dueling applied, but Martin Bellock wasn't a guy who fought with honor. He'd go all the way, if the opening presented itself.

I couldn't let him do that. I couldn't let him take me away from Tresten, and from my family.

* * *

Tresten's hand on my shoulder jerked me awake. I looked around, bewildered. I was still sitting cross-legged in the middle of the floor.

"I fell asleep," I said. "Shit. What time is it?"

"Time to get ready," he said.

"Are you okay?" I asked him. "Were you able to sleep?"

He nodded. "Barely. I'm sorry I wasn't here to help you last night."

I stood up and squeezed his hand. "I needed to be by myself, I think."

"How do you feel?" I could sense that what he really wanted to ask was *will you be alright?*

"Like shit," I said, smiling. "I'll be fine."

Rain continued to come down in thick sheets that drummed against the car as we drove to the Dawn Academy. The match would be held in the FAS training gym under the witness of our families, the pack leaders, and the judgement of Master Graffer.

There was a small group gathered outside the entrance of the FAS main hall, and when we made our way up I realized that they were my classmates—my friends and guys who I'd trained with. A lot of them had become distant after it came out that Tresten and I were together. They were all of the mindset—the same one that I'd had before—that an omega was out of place in the FAS.

Soaked from standing in the rain, they stopped us at the entrance and Jackson VanKrennick stepped forward. "Loch, Tresten," he said. "I just want you both to know that we're all behind you. Martin and his family have gone on too long with their dog shit, and we're glad someone is stepping up to them."

"Martin's gang was planning on being a nuisance here," Stell Lenford said. "They planned on showing up to fuck with you here. But we took care of them."

I nodded to them. "Thank you, guys. Be careful, though. We don't want this spiraling out of hand and causing trouble for your families."

"We'll be fine. Good luck to you, Loch. Kick his ass for us."

. . .

Inside the training arena, seats had been arranged around the circular perimeter for the spectators. The families had already gathered there, with the Crocs and Lunas on one side and the Bellocks on the opposite. The ground at the center of the arena had turned muddy from the rain that fell in through the open circle in the roof, and a steady curtain of water continued to patter down into wide, murky puddles of reddish brown muck.

I greeted our family, each member giving me a hug. Van had a set of crutches with him, and I kept him from standing up to greet me. "How you doing, bro?" I asked him.

"Looking forward to seeing you stomp that Bellock into the mud," he said. "And I'm stoked to be in *the* FAS training gym. This place is *awesome*."

Dad grabbed my bicep, squeezed, then nodded. Then he took me by the shoulder and looked me in the eyes. "Where does a wolf of honor, strength, and pride tread?"

"Beneath the Crescent Moon," I replied.

He nodded. "Go and win."

Tresten took my hand, his ice blue eyes searching mine. We pressed our foreheads together, and I could feel his strength. We didn't say anything to each other—we didn't need to.

WED TO THE OMEGA

Everything that needed to be said was contained in the way we looked at each other.

"Fighters!" Master Graffer said, entering the ring. "Take your positions. Let's get this over with."

I left Tresten and walked to the center of the arena, stripping off my robes and tossing them aside. The rain fell straight down there, looking like a portal into another world. I stepped through the curtain of water to join Master Graffer and Martin there, my body immediately drenched and dripping. The mud clung to me with every step.

Martin stood with a slight smirk on his face, his dangerously vacant eyes staring down at me. His hair was matted across his forehead like tentacles, his fists clenched at his side. His eyes flicked over my shoulder before returning to mine. I knew who he was looking at—Tresten. His smirk widened into a putrid grin, and he licked his lips.

My vision trembled, and I felt the heat of anger rising up in me. *Control,* I thought. *You've got this.*

"This is what you've trained for," Master Graffer said. "This is no training match. All is allowed, but you are not to make a killing blow. Fight with honor. The terms of the match are clear. Are you ready?"

. . .

We both nodded, our eyes locked.

Your mind is clear.

"Salute."

I clasped my palm over my fist in front of me. Martin refused to return the gesture.

"Bellock, salute," Master Graffer said. Martin grunted and spat on the ground. Master Graffer exhaled, and then stepped back.

"Ready? *Fight!*"

My wolf dashed out from the deep recesses of my soul, howling towards the crescent moon. My body shook as all my bones did their dance to reorder. Martin would no doubt go half-wolf where his brute strength was, so I would go full to boost my agility and senses.

I pushed my hands out as I fell forward, and when they hit the mud they were paws. My ears pushed up, my tail out, my fangs lengthening into brutal sabers. I exploded forward through the muck, and I saw Martin's eyes widen in surprise. He was still shifting, just making it to the half-wolf point.

. . .

Fuck you, I thought, and snapped my jaws shut. The hot, metallic taste of blood filled my mouth.

He roared in pain. I landed behind him and tossed his severed ear to the ground.

He whirled, holding one clawed hand to his bleeding head, and charged at me. His eyes were wild with fury. He swung a boulder of a fist at me, but I easily dodged to the side and his strike bashed into the ground. His arm sunk all the way up to his wrist. I wasn't going to waste this opportunity. I leapt—

Martin turned, and my vision went black as needles of pain shot through my eyes. Martin had yanked his hand free and hurled mud right into them. I couldn't see. I landed, trying to shake the mud from my eyes, but it was thick and caked onto my face.

I heard him coming, nearly too late. I dodged and pranced backward, holding my face up to the rain to try and wash the mud away. I could smell him coming. I dodged again, but this time a sear of pain caught my side.

"I'm going to kill you!" he roared. "I'm going to tear you to pieces, you omega loving piece of shit!"

I felt a rise of panic. My vision was a blur. The only way I could clear it off completely would be to shift back to half-shift form, but I couldn't take that risk. I'd be open, completely vulnerable.

Clear your mind.

Trust your intuition.

Balance.

I still had my smell and my hearing. I didn't need to see.

I stopped trying to see, and closed my eyes. I straightened, alert, listening. The sound of the rain pattered on the ground, muddling things. I focused, isolating the sound. I sniffed the air.

A clear image of everything formed in my mind to an extent that I'd never reached before. I was hyper aware of everything. I could "see" Martin pacing around me, readying his attack. I heard his muscles contracting. I smelled the dirty anger emanating from his body. I could even hear the sound of his lips curling into that stupid smirk of his.

He dashed forward at me—he was going to try and make a blow for my left shoulder.

. . .

No honor at all.

I heard every footstep and saw the path of his strike. I stepped aside and he stumbled forward, landing face first into the mud. Cursing, he got up and came around. I dodged him again, this time tripping him with my back paw. He howled in pain and frustration as the open wound where his ear used to be smashed into the mud. He came up again. And again. Each time, I dodged him easily. My mind was focused, completely in tune with my body and my heart.

"I could do this all day," I said. "You're never going to touch me, Martin."

He let out a crazed, furious roar that didn't sound like it was from a shifter. He sounded like a wild animal.

He came at me for the last time. This time, when he hugged the dirt, I leapt onto his back and grabbed his neck in my jaws. With just a flinch of a muscle, I could've ended him right there. He froze.

"Match! That's a match. Killing blow from Loch!"

"Stay down," I growled to him. He snorted furiously into the mud, blood streaming over his face from his wound, his eye swiveling around madly.

. . .

I stepped back, and Master Graffer rushed in to separate us. "That's it."

I only then realized how fast my heart was pounding in my chest, and the rest of the world seemed to come back to me. I shifted back to human form, and when I wiped away the mud from my eyes, the first thing I saw was Tresten running towards me, his arms spread wide. He broke through the wall of rain and leapt at me, and I caught him in my arms.

Martin's father, who looked remarkably similar to him and maybe twice as ugly, came and picked his son up off the ground, grabbing him by the wrist.

"I'll fucking get you, Loch," Martin spat, straining against his father's grasp. "I'm going to fucking *get you—*" He yelped in shock as his father's palm smacked against his face.

"Shut your mouth, boy. You've embarrassed us enough." He snatched up Martin's ear from the ground.

"You were *incredible*," Tresten said. "I could hardly believe what I was seeing." He kissed me.

"Thought I was going to get my ass kicked?" I said, smiling into our kiss.

. . .

"Your technique," he said. "That was *master* level fighting, Loch. Pa even said it. You should've seen him and your dad. Their mouths were on the floor."

"It was your training," I said. "It clicked. The moment I squared off against him, I knew this was do or die, and it all fell into place." I hugged him close. "I would've been nowhere without you, Tresten. Nowhere."

We kissed again, the rain falling down around us.

As the adrenaline faded and my mind slowed, I suddenly felt exhausted—and also relieved. I'd won the fight, and defended my husband and our family's honor. This challenge was over, but I realized that the two of us were only at the start of the next challenge.

I held Tresten against me, and he rested his forehead against mine. We were together. I slid my hand around to his front and pressed it to his stomach. This was only the start of our adventures together. This was just the beginning of our love.

EPILOGUE - TRESTEN

The sky above was filled with glittering stars, and a brisk wind ruffled my robe. The ceremony was conducted on a hill that overlooked the Dawn Academy, next to the ruins of what used to be a guard tower dating back to the era when the school was first constructed. I shivered, and looked over towards the crowd, worrying if Ian was cold too.

He was sitting next to Loch, his hand in his father's, kicking his little legs as they hung over the edge of the chair. He looked bored, and I didn't blame him. Sitting still and watching a long and quiet ceremony was the last thing an energetic little five-year-old omega like him would want to do. I'd had the toughest time teaching him the meditation lessons my father had showed me when I was his age—all Ian wanted to do was scamper around in his wolf form. He was more like Loch, in that regard.

. . .

I smiled, watching as Loch leaned over and kissed him on his head. He ruffled our son's white hair and whispered something in his ear. Ian burst into a fit of giggles, his blue eyes flashing brightly even in the dim light of the torches.

"Next, we'd like to congratulate Tresten Croc Luna," said Master Graffer. The crowd applauded, and I stood up and joined him on the platform. Ian stopped fidgeting and looked up at me, his eyes wide. I gave him a little wave, and he grinned.

"Tresten has always been one of the best at the Fighting Arts School during his years here, and one of my most skilled students. When the call of duty to his family came, I was uncertain whether he would be able to complete his training —but he did, doing everything he could from his home to keep his skills sharp. When he returned to the Fighting Arts School, I expected to need to retrain him—but found a warrior who was even stronger than he was when he'd taken his leave. Now, I'm proud to bestow an honor to Tresten Croc Luna well-fitting of his abilities as a fighter."

Master Graffer turned to me. "Tresten, please shift."

I closed my eyes and soon was standing in my wolf form, still draped in my black robes.

"Tresten Croc Luna. You are hereby granted the rank of master fighter. You stand alongside the great masters of the

Fighting Arts School and the Dawn Academy who came before, and still breathe on today, alphas, betas—and omegas. Make your call to the world."

I tilted my head back to the moon and let loose a long howl into the sky. The crowd erupted into applause. When I returned to my human form, I looked and saw everyone was standing for me. Ian jumped off his seat and ran towards me, and Loch followed him, a wide grin on his face. I smiled, and made my way down from the platform towards the warm embrace of my family.

Thank you so much for reading! To access **exclusive bonus material**, keep turning to the very end of the book!

And if you enjoyed *Wed to the Omega*, please consider leaving a rating or review. All positive encouragement is a great help to authors! You can easily access the product page by scanning the QR code.

KEEP IN TOUCH WITH ASHE

Stay updated with sales and new releases by subscribing to Ashe Moon's personal newsletter. Scan the QR code below with your phone camera!

* * *

If you're looking for something a little more personal you can also join my private Facebook group, **Ashe Moon's Ashetronauts**!

My group is a safe space to chat with me and other readers, and where I also do special exclusive giveaways and announcements. Hope to see you there!

NEXT IN THE SERIES...

Vander Luna refused to accept the traditional omega lifestyle —find an alpha, pop out a few kids… No, he was going to be a *warrior*. When Vander fails at his one shot to get into the world's best fighting school, what else does he have left? Despite his parent's wishes, settling down with a man is the very last thing on Vander's mind—but when he gets lost trekking through snow-covered bear territory, it seems fate has other plans for him.

For bears, the two worst things you can do are associate with wolves, and forsake the family business—and Pell Darkclaw has done both. A talented doctor, Pell abandoned his small clan to volunteer his skills in the wolf towns in desperate need of good healers. When he finds Vander lost and freezing in a snowstorm, Pell takes him in to nurse him back to health. The storm means no one is leaving Pell's cozy little cabin any time soon. Just what can happen when a wounded wolf omega and a protective bear alpha are snowed in alone together?

Vander's Story - Doctor to the Omega
Christophe's Story - Marked to the Omega
Arthur's Story - Bound to the Omega

Also From Ashe Moon

*"A surprising adventure and decisions affect more than one life and the town. Great story. **Absolutely wonderful characters.**"*

Pregnant and without an alpha, human omega Grayson must rely on his tenacity to provide for his unborn daughter. But when a fire claims his home and everything he's struggled to work for, rescue comes in an unexpected form: the alpha dragon Altair and his flight of firefighters who reluctantly take Grayson into their custody.

Altair's resentment of humanity is matched by a conflicting sense of duty to protect the town they share and all who call it home, human or dragon. He and his flight brothers have never had to deal with an omega before—let alone a human—and now they have one living under their roof! Everything Altair thought he knew about humans, omegas, and mates is called into question—and with Grayson's baby on the way, he's about to find out what it's like to be a daddy.

Daddy From Flames is the first book in the Dragon

Firefighters mpreg series. This book features dragon shifters, a human omega, firefighters, an industrial fantasy setting, pregnancy/birth, new dads, a cat, love healing wounds, action, fun, light drama, and, as always, a happily ever after.

Scan the QR code with your phone camera to see the entire series!

FREE BONUS MATERIAL

Sign up for my mailing list and receive the **FREE bonus material** for *Wed to the Omega*.

FREE BONUS MATERIAL

First edition cover

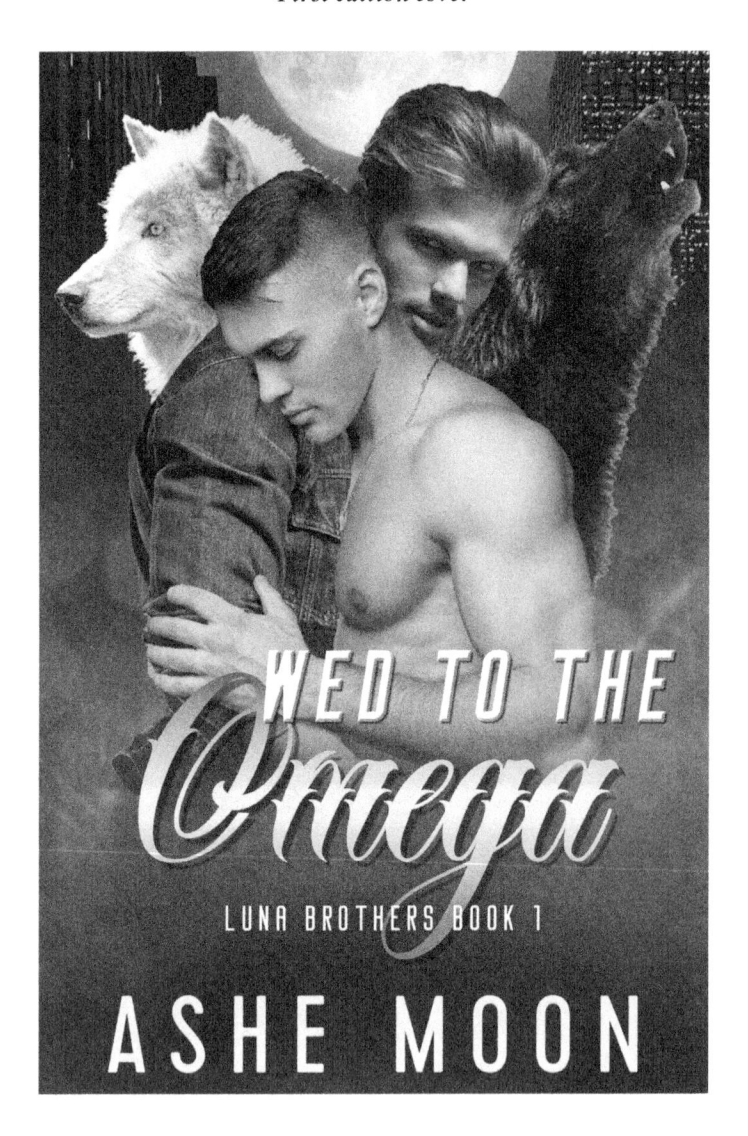